FRANKIE

DOMINI HIGHSMITH

FRANKIE

BANTAM PRESS

LONDON · NEW YORK · TORONTO · SYDNEY · AUCKLAND

TRANSWORLD PUBLISHERS LTD
61-63 Uxbridge Road, London W5 5SA

TRANSWORLD PUBLISHERS (AUSTRALIA)
PTY LTD
15-23 Helles Avenue, Moorebank, NSW 2170

TRANSWORLD PUBLISHERS (NZ) LTD
Cnr Moselle and Waipareira Aves,
Henderson, Auckland

Published 1990 by Bantam Press
a division of Transworld Publishers Ltd
Copyright © Domini Wiles 1990

The right of Domini Wiles to be identified as the author
of this work has been asserted in accordance with
section 77 and 78 of the Copyright Designs and Patents
Act 1988

British Library Cataloguing in Publication Data
Highsmith, Domini
  Frankie.
  I. Title
  833'.914 [J]

ISBN 0-593-01939-3

Typeset by Chippendale Type, Otley, West Yorkshire.
Printed in Great Britain by Biddles Ltd, Guildford
and Kings Lynn.

This book is dedicated

to my brother, Duke
to my sister, Melodie

and to Tony, who made it possible

1

FRANKIE DID NOT WANT to think of his mam and the Irishman. He hated Big Tom Fish, with his cruel jokes and flashing green eyes and rough workman's hands. He screwed his eyes tightly shut and tried not to imagine what they were doing together in the room with the shuttered window.

Although he was nine years old and would soon be moving up to the big school, Frankie was still frightened of the dark. It sucked all warmth and courage from his body, leaving him chilled to the bone and fearful of even the smallest movement in the big house. Shivering, he picked his way down the draughty main staircase to the unlit hall, guided by the grunting and moaning sounds coming from the sitting-room. He had been crouched on the first-floor landing for a long time, peering through the banister rails to the kitchen at the end of the lower corridor, listening to the ebb and flow of their conversation. He had heard their laughter, their long silences and the chink of their wine-glasses one against the other. Then he had watched them walk to the main room with their arms around each other and kiss in the warm light before closing the door behind them. He did not want to believe that it was so, but he had to know for certain. He had to see it for himself.

He groped his way through the shadows at the foot of the stairs, located the large brass handle and turned it with both hands. The door opened on to a glittering, brightly lit room crammed with antique furniture, *objets d'art* and exotic bric-à-brac. Here were swords and rapiers hanging from sashes on panelled walls, delicate figurines set on marble pedestals, statues from across the far China seas, carved elephants and lions from Africa, Javanese dancing girls with jointed limbs, fierce ceremonial masks from the mountains of Indonesia. Here, too, were stuffed crocodiles with needle-like teeth, deadly blow-pipes from the Amazon jungle and glittering brasswork from Burma and Arabia and Ceylon. A log fire crackled and spat in the grate, sending flickers of light across rugs and draperies fashioned with threads of purest silk. This was the best room, the Aladdin's cave forbidden to all but his parents, the place where wondrous treasures were kept behind locked doors and heavily shuttered windows. Frankie blinked in the bright light, then turned his gaze reluctantly to the arched alcove on his left. There was the weighted velvet curtain that had once hung in the Star Theatre, now fixed to a huge rod with rings so large that Frankie could slip them over his arms like bangles. There was the big brass bed with its snowy white sheets, its marshmallow pillows and top-cover of fringed ivory lace. He blinked again and shivered from head to toe. Despite his terror of darkness and subterranean places, he wanted the ground to open at his feet and swallow him into its blackest hole.

She lay across the big bed with her head thrown back so that her long hair fell like a veil of copper across the coverlet. She was naked. Her breasts were crushed and pinched by callused fingers, her thighs lifted to meet the demands of the muscular buttocks thrusting against her. She was lying there without protest, her flesh quivering beneath the weight of the man who lay grunting and sweating between her legs.

The boy swallowed the lump that had risen to his

8

throat. Her face was fixed with a strange expression, eyes open, lips parted. She seemed to be staring back at him with a smile that was almost a grimace of pain yet somehow full of mockery. Tears of outrage stung his eyes, and something deeper than humiliation sank like a stone into the pit of his stomach. This was not one of the women he had peeped at on other occasions. This was not chubby Eileen with the blue-veined legs, or black-skinned Blossom with the frizzy wire-wool hair. Nor was it some stranger come to drink and dance and lie with a man in a borrowed bed. This was his beautiful lady, his Sweetheart. It made him feel sick to his soul to watch the naked Irishman snorting with pleasure on his mam's bed.

He closed the door again with a soft click, shutting out the room's light and plunging the hallway back into blackness. On leaden feet he moved back to the staircase and made his way to the half-landing at its top. There the panelled walls and worn linoleum were faintly illuminated by a rectangle of grey light from the frosted glass in the bathroom door. He sat down on one of the bare wooden steps. Once his eyes became accustomed to the gloom he was able to make out the double curve of the banister as it snaked from the dark first-floor landing into the inky blackness of the main stairwell. To his right a shorter flight of steps gave access to an equally dark corridor along which he must walk to reach his bedroom. It led past the scarred brown door of the Bogeyman's room, where strange noises and unpleasant smells were constant reminders of danger. At his back, the glow from an outside lamp found its way through curtained windows to touch the glazed bathroom door with an eerie greyness. Standing in a corner of the half-landing was an old mirror with chipped edges: a tall narrow sheet of glass that had once been pinned to the inside of a wardrobe door. Now

9

its painted side was crumbling, falling away in patches that left irregular silver stains like a weird mould growing within the glass. On certain nights the mirror had a faint lustre that separated it from the deeper shadows of the corner in which it stood. Even when it was too dark to see anything reflected there, the suggestion of movement within the tainted glass gave added weight to the boy's night-time fears.

Frankie was shivering. He was wearing only a sleeveless vest and a pair of short pants that reached almost to his bony knees. Although not nearly so cold as the ceramic tiles of the hall, the linoleum beneath his bare feet had a chill that seemed to creep right through his body. His dark head was bowed. He was weeping quietly, allowing the tears to run down his cheeks and drip into the dusty shadows around his feet. It was a long time before his sobs subsided, and by then other, less ugly sounds were coming from the room downstairs. He heard a man's gruff voice and a loud slap, followed by familiar lilting laughter. Her gaiety only served to increase his distress. It somehow belittled him.

Tom Fish was a very tall man with big hands and a cruel sense of humour. He took a sadistic delight in teasing the boy for his nervousness, taunting him because he was so small for his age and very thin. He called him a skinny runt and a half-grown whelp, and he bellowed with amusement whenever a threatening movement or a deliberately sudden yell of 'Boo' caused the boy to flinch with alarm. Now Frankie listened to the rumble of the Irishman's voice down there in the darkness and he wished him dead. More than anything else in the world, he wanted to see that muscular hairy body hanging from a bloody meat-hook in the cellar among the turkey carcasses and slaughtered pigs.

The house called Old Ashfield contained seventeen

rooms above ground and a labyrinth of cellars built around an ancient underground well. Its large terraced gardens formed but a part of six and a half acres of land enclosed on three sides by high walls and locked gates. Most of the walls were topped by a layer of concrete into which were set jagged pieces of glass from smashed bottles. Strangers were rarely seen on that private and closely guarded property. Neither the present occupants nor their noisy assortment of animals extended any kind of welcome to trespassers.

At its front the land dropped down through gardens and woodland to lower slopes choked with thornbushes and tangled weed. Beyond the perimeter wall ran a vein of the Bradford Beck, its filthy waters gurgling below ground before breaking free for some distance to pass Old Ashfield's wooded hillside. Then it rushed into a low tunnel, gathering factory and household waste on its long journey to the main flow of the beck near the town centre. On a few occasions Frankie had found the courage to scale the perimeter wall to look for rats in the mouth of the tunnel. He had never actually seen one, but he knew they were there. He had heard their scurrying feet and noisy squeaks, and he had been forced to nip his nostrils closed against their foul stench. Rats were disgusting creatures. They lived in filth and fed on shit and vomit and rotting flesh. One of the boys at school knew a kid whose father worked with a man whose cousin died of rabies after being bitten by a rat from Bradford Beck. They went for the throat or the genitals, and the smallest scratch from their long black claws could poison a man to death.

There was a pipe jutting through the stone wall at the tunnel's mouth, a wide cast-iron duct that brought nasty stuff all the way down the hillside from the great well in the cellar under the stairs. On slaughtering days all the gates were carefully locked and a long wooden ramp placed against the cellar steps. The doomed pigs were grabbed by their hind legs and forced to run on tip-toe down the sloping backyard or along the crazy paving on the front terrace. They went through the house like so many screaming wheelbarrows, soon to be silenced by men with sharp knives and rubber aprons and boots that did not slip on the bloodied floor. On such days Frankie had watched the water in the beck change from dirty brown to a rich deep red. There were even times when the massive outlet-pipe became blocked at the point where it burst from the hillside and through the tunnel wall. Then someone would have to wade into the mouth of the tunnel with a hooked stick to pull out the blockage so that the blood could run away freely. He was not allowed to mention the slaughtering to anyone, not even as a special secret between best friends. It had something to do with the black market and ration-books and the Men From The Ministry.

The spacious stone house had originally been one of three sharing the same hilly and thickly wooded parcel of land. Too run-down and curiously situated to appeal to most families, it had stood empty for several years before Frankie's parents made it their home. One particular disadvantage was the fact that its immediate neighbours had been allowed to crumble into decay, leaving Frankie's home sandwiched between two boarded, dilapidated buildings barely fit for storage. Apart from a small stepped garden directly in front of the house, the grounds were neglected and overgrown, making the terrace steps difficult to negotiate and allowing grass to undermine the paving stones on the long front terrace. Bushes of prickly blackberry and wild rose had broken free of the lower level and were now marching towards the house like an insidious green army. On the upper slopes the peonies shared their ground with fireweed and there were tall purple-headed thistles standing among the irises. In many places the wild greenery formed a natural barrier through which even the dogs were unable to pass. Old Ashfield was a place of many secrets, a private world neatly encapsulated within its own high walls. Only sometimes, on very quiet nights, could Frankie hear the hum of traffic or the distant chiming of the Town Hall clock to remind him that a whole city existed beyond the locked gates.

'Sweetheart. Sweetheart.' He whispered the name softly, then sniffed and wiped the dampness from his nose and upper lip with the back of his hand. Even after all this time, her name sounded strange to his ears. He wanted to call her 'Mam', the way he had a long time ago, but she said it made her feel middle-aged and dull and ordinary, so he must never say it again, especially when other people were around. The sudden change had not come easy to him, and even now he found himself muttering 'Mam' under his breath because that old name was somehow special and precious. On those rare occasions when it slipped out accidentally, her rage was a clear indication of how deeply his carelessness pained her. She was Sweetheart. She was younger and more beautiful and much more clever than any other mother, and she told her friends that Frankie had chosen the name all by himself to prove just how much he loved her. He wanted very much for her to know how much he loved her, so he had called her 'Mam', then 'Angel', and now 'Sweetheart', because it made her happy.

On the darkened half-landing Frankie rubbed his face to wipe away the last of his tears. He was very cold. The room downstairs had grown quiet, yet still the Irishman had not emerged. In his mind's eye he saw them together in the brass-ended bed, his lovely Sweetheart with her silky hair and creamy-white skin, and beside her the grinning Tom Fish with one more cruel weapon to use against a little boy.

Frankie got to his feet and tip-toed up the steps to the first-floor landing. A faint sliver of light showed along the bottom of the door on his right. He held his breath, listening for any sound to indicate that the Bogeyman was standing in the gloom, waiting to pounce. Sweetheart knew about these things. She knew that the Bogeyman was a huge bat-like creature who lived in dark corners and feasted on the blood of ungrateful and disobedient children. Only she could protect him from its hungry clutches. She took good care of him. She always warned him, in whispered anxious tones, whenever the Bogeyman was on the prowl. Tonight she had said nothing, so Frankie almost believed himself safe, yet he lived with the constant fear that one night she would make a horrible mistake and he would walk to his death in the inky shadows upstairs.

His room lay at the very end of the corridor, beyond the locked doors of closets and bedrooms and attic steps. Keeping his gaze on the thread of light seeping out from the Bogeyman's room, he inched his way along the threadbare strip of carpet. A smell peculiar to that place assailed his nostrils with its pungency. He hugged the banister, counting its bar-like wooden rods until he reached the turn where it met the wall. Then he ran, plunging into a tunnel of darkness less fearful than the imagined horrors lurking behind that heavy dark-brown door.

Frankie climbed into bed, curled himself into a tight ball and pulled the covers up over his head. His teeth were chattering. As warmth slowly enveloped his body the spasms of shivering increased. It was a long time before they subsided sufficiently for him to relax his muscles and lie still in the rough familiar comfort of tangled blankets. A feeling of nausea had settled in his stomach, leaving a sour taste at the back of his throat that no amount of swallowing would take away. It was all his fault. This hateful thing had taken place, and Frankie knew that somehow he must be to blame. Even as he drifted into sleep, his eyes pricked with unshed tears and his mind was filled with images of the Irishman snorting like a foraging pig around his mam's naked body.

2

FRANKIE WOKE with a start. One of the dogs was barking. That would be Rosie, the brindle Great Dane. Her temper had worsened since the pups were born, so now she had to be kept tied up all the time in the alcove near the kitchen stove. He raised his head to listen. The barking ended on a sudden, very loud howl. Somewhere in the house a door slammed. A chink of light from behind the thick curtain told him that it was morning, and the prospect brought with it a deep sense of foreboding. He had witnessed a bad thing last night. It had seemed to him that her eyes looked right into his as he stood in the darkened hall, staring into the room. He had even imagined that she mocked him with her smile, though he could not be certain that she had actually *seen* him there. If she had, he would surely be punished for leaving his room and daring to open her private door. His fate would depend entirely upon her mood, which he knew from experience could shift and change in the winking of an eye.

He could hear the man moving about in the room above his own. Heavy footsteps crossed the ceiling from corner to corner, striding back and forth, to and fro in a familiar monotonous pattern. It was the mindless pacing of a caged animal. The man had a rasping cough that exploded from his lungs in noisy barks which often left him groaning and gasping for breath. Sometimes in the night he cried out in a hoarse voice and moaned as if struggling to escape the grip of

16

a bad dream. And sometimes he wept. It seemed to Frankie that he had been up there, locked in the smallest of the attic rooms, for a long time.

It was thanks to the man upstairs that Frankie had acquired the enormous army greatcoat with its fancy epaulettes and polished brass buttons. The stranger had arrived in the dead of night, a sick man unable to walk unaided and noisily man-handled through the darkened house by several other men. In the confusion his greatcoat had slipped to the floor, where it lay unnoticed by all but the ever-watchful child. Now it belonged to Frankie, and while he secretly warmed himself in its folds he spared little thought for the comfort of its previous owner.

The boy slept in a large front bedroom whose window, were it not so closely covered by an old woollen blanket, looked out over the once elegant front walkway with its crazy paving and stepped terraces. There were trees outside, great towering hulks of oak, ash and chestnut that stood almost as tall as the house itself. On windy nights they tapped at the windows with woody fingers. When it rained their branches swayed and hissed with a sound like that of the ocean spilling over some distant shore. Last summer Frankie had climbed the tallest ash and found himself in a whole new world. From its leafy canopy he could see right over the gardens and the wilderness of the lower grounds to the rows of cobbled streets on the far side of the beck wall. Beyond them other streets with narrow rear alleyways and outside lavatories stretched all the way to the main road. He recognized the church of St Andrew with its high spire and the nearby school with its iron railings and tiny concrete playgrounds. Closer to home were the squat red-brick piggeries, the turkey-huts and chicken-houses, the litter of sheds and lean-tos where he was not allowed to play. He could see the long walkway below

17

him, the small iron gates at each end with steps leading down to both sides of the house. He had remained in the tree for a long time, cramped and a little nervous, yet totally fascinated. He had climbed so high that he could see damaged slates on the roof of the house and sections of guttering choked with leaves and other debris. Then had come the shock of seeing a face peering out at him from the attic window. One moment he had thought himself alone amongst the greenery and the next he was staring into grey gaunt features closely framed by a tiny skylight in the angle of the roof. The face was long and pale, with a shaggy beard and eyes that seemed to look out from deep hollows. The lips were moving, shaping words that had no sound. For long moments Frankie was held as if transfixed by the man's gaze. Then fear overcame curiosity and he scrambled down from the tree with such haste that he skinned his knees and gouged a long deep gash along the inside of his forearm. He could still recall the sense of dread that hung over him for days as he waited to be thrashed for that escapade. He would never understand why the man in the attic had not betrayed him.

In a corner of Frankie's room stood a large wooden chest whose drawers were too stiff for him to open. Its hanging brass handles were damaged and tarnished, its once polished top ruined by years of misuse. The linoleum beside the chest was badly stained by spills from the big white pot where he relieved himself at night when the house was very quiet and scary. No matter how he tried, he could not judge exactly when to empty the pot before it became too heavy for him to carry all the way to the bathroom. His room had a smell that could be found nowhere else in the house. It was a damp musty smell. It reminded him of dogs with wet coats, or very old people, or mouse droppings.

There was a large brown wardrobe standing against

the wall with a block of wood supporting one of its damaged feet. Its doors were locked. Someone had trapped folded paper in the bottom drawer and removed the handles so it could no longer be opened except, perhaps, by a very strong man. The long space between wardrobe and window was piled high with unwanted furniture, broken chairs, boxes, old gardening tools and stacks of old newspapers. He slept alone in the big double bed, curled up in his stolen greatcoat beneath a single woollen blanket exactly like the one that was nailed across the window. Sometimes he wet himself when he was distressed in the night, or when he slept too deeply to heed the warning pains of a full bladder. Then he would move to another part of the bed, away from the cold wet patch that would take a long time to dry and leave a stiff yellow stain on the mattress. Nobody ever came into Frankie's room, not even his parents. It was *his* room, his very own private bedroom. Sweetheart told him he must never forget how lucky he was. She said he must be the only nine-year-old boy in the whole of Yorkshire who had a proper bedroom all to himself.

Under his bed was rolled a piece of carpet with a fringed edge, and among its creases Frankie kept his treasures. Here was his beloved Mr Ted, the battered, forbidden stuffed bear that Sweetheart had wanted to consign to the bonfire. Here, too, were knick-knacks and glossy magazines stolen from some of the other rooms: a leather belt with a carved brass buckle that shone like gold when polished with a cloth, a brooch set with brilliant red and yellow stones, an airman's badge, a pen-knife, a fountain pen. In a strong khaki handkerchief he kept his money, the handful of coins he had managed to save or pilfer and hide away in spite of Sweetheart's threats that she would always find him out if he tried to lie or keep wicked secrets from her. This was his real treasure. One day he would be wealthy enough to buy shoes with metal caps and a fur-lined leather jacket, and a big iron skillet filled to the brim with red meat and eggs and mushrooms and sausages and crispy fried bread in sizzling hot fat.

The last item in his concealed hoard was an airtight biscuit-tin whose hinged lid bore a picture of the Old Queen in black mourning robes. Inside the tin were several small parcels containing measured portions of custard powder and porridge oats, crushed biscuits and cocoa powder mixed with sugar. Frankie had learned to prepare in advance for those days and nights when he might otherwise go hungry.

Although he had always feared the night, the boy knew the big house in darkness almost as well as in daylight. He recognized each draught of icy air slicing through cracks in doors made invisible by crowding shadows. His bare feet could identify all the frayed patches on the long ribbon of carpet and each worn tread on the stairs. He knew the feel of every cold stone step on the wide staircase leading down to the main hall. There were no lights except in the downstairs rooms, so he had learned to hold his breath against the muddy darkness to prevent it reaching into his lungs to suffocate him. Even in the dead of night this was Frankie's house. He knew its sounds and smells, its forbidden places and inky-black corners. He had learned to live with its many secrets and its brooding sense of menace.

The man in the attic was coughing again. A faint smell of frying bacon drifted up from the kitchen. It drew the hungry child from his bed to the landing, where he glanced nervously at the Bogeyman's room before creeping on tip-toe along the strip of faded carpet. When he crouched in the gap between the attic door and the first curve of the banister, he could look through the rails and see right along the ground-floor corridor to the kitchen. The door was open. Both dogs were straining at their chains, Rosie trampling her five pups and drooling at the mouth, Lady pawing the air with her front feet in a begging gesture. They, too, were hungry.

He could see Big Tom Fish hunched over a large plate of food, and he recalled afresh, in agonizing detail, the broad naked back and the strong buttocks working between his mother's legs. He wondered if the Irishman had been surprised by the roughness of her nipples and the prickly coarseness of her pubic hair against his skin.

Frankie remained crouched on the landing until the man in the kitchen pushed his plate aside and wiped the back of his hand across his mouth. A large mug of tea vanished in a single gulp, then the man and woman moved out of sight towards the outer door in the kitchen's lower corner. It was some time before the door opened and closed in a muffle of lowered voices.

Sweetheart was alone when she came back into view, and Frankie could not recall when he had seen her look more beautiful. She twirled and swayed around the room in a slow dance, her skirts billowing and her long hair shining beneath the bright lights. With her hands she smoothed the front of her blouse until her breasts swelled against the top button. Her skin was almost as white and silky as the fabric itself. She was happy. Her eyes were closed, and she was smiling. Just watching her made Frankie feel warm inside. Last year she had come to his school for the first time, and every eye had turned to gape at her long red hair and golden earrings as she swept into the assembly-hall wearing one of her special dresses. Frankie had felt enormously proud. No other boy had such a mother. She was just like a movie star. While other mams wore sensible shoes and coats of grey or dark brown, Sweetheart dazzled the world in crimson skirts and fabulous coats trimmed with genuine leopard fur. She wore American silk stockings embossed with beads and flowers, coloured leather shoes with high heels and peek-a-boo toes, and multi-shaded scarves tied gypsy-fashion around her hair. He did not even care when the teachers stared and some of the bigger boys made rude jokes about her shapely legs and body. She had warned him to be wary of the coarse and petty jealousies of common people. She was above them all. She shimmered and shone like a precious jewel, a princess. Frankie watched her now with a mixture of awe and delight as she pranced in little pirouettes around the kitchen. She must surely be the most beautiful woman in the whole world.

After a while she closed the kitchen door without calling Frankie for breakfast. Knowing he must never go downstairs without permission, he tip-toed back to his room to wait. There he lifted a corner of the curtain to peer out at the bright patches of daylight filtering through the trees. He was thinking about school dinners and salty cabbage when he heard her other voice, her harsh, cold, angry voice, screeching from the hallway downstairs.

'Frankie! Frankie! What the hell do you think you're doing up there, you snivelling little brat? Get yourself down here. Get down here this minute!'

Her anger sliced through him like a knife. He could tell by the tone of her voice that today she would be counting, and woe betide him if he failed to reach the kitchen before his allotted twenty seconds were used up. With his heart pounding in his chest and with barely a glance at the dreaded Bogeyman's door, he raced along the landing and down the main stairs. He paused only to smooth down his unruly black hair and tuck his vest into his pants before groping his way down the long dark corridor to the kitchen door.

3

THE KITCHEN was a large stone-floored room whose low ceiling seemed to trap the heat of the stove and hold cooking smells long after the meal that created them had been forgotten. The outer door was set into the lower corner of the left-hand wall. It opened on to a flagged walled yard that sloped steeply upward to where steps and a battered gate gave access to the rear driveway, with its ramshackle collection of goat- and poultry-pens. A window over the deep pot sink looked out on the upper part of the yard, its panes of dusty glass still criss-crossed with scraps of air-raid tape several years after the end of the war. Its woodwork had softened and split in a number of places, and the once rich velvet of its drapes was now faded in patches and spotted with household stains. Opposite the window, a coal-burning stove with a chimney stood in the centre of an alcove originally designed to accommodate a massive Victorian cooking range. There were several hot-water pipes leading off from the stove, heated rails where wet clothes were hung to dry and plates of food were left to keep warm after serving. Sometimes Buddie stacked trays of eggs above the pipes to incubate, and after a few days there would be dozens of fluffy, chirruping chicks hatching out in the heat. Like the fire in the best room, the kitchen stove was kept burning day and night, winter and summer. Sweetheart hated the cold.

Tethered in the deep spaces on either side of the stove

were the two dogs, Lady and Rosie, one a short-sighted bulldog of uncertain temperament, the other a bloody-minded Great Dane bent on demolishing or devouring everything that came within reach of her snapping teeth. Rosie was particularly hostile to the boy. She seemed to sense his nervousness. His very presence was sufficient to have her barking in rage or baring her teeth in threatening snarls. Her recently born pups were five helpless whimpering bundles curled in the dirty sacking at her feet. Rosie was an indifferent mother. Her care of the pups was so haphazard that Buddie often fed them milk from a baby's bottle to make sure they were getting enough nourishment. Frankie did not like the dogs. They fouled their corners and filled the hot room with their smells, and they frightened him with their incessant snarling. Rosie had bitten him twice in the past; once when she managed to free herself by chewing through her tethering-rope, and once when she leaped through the window of Buddie's jeep and chased him into the pig-yard. He still bore the scars of her teeth on his calf and upper thigh. Lady was old and followed the Great Dane's example because she was too stupid to know any better. Left alone she was so docile that she ignored Frankie completely, but in the company of the ferocious Rosie she, too, became a dangerous animal. Now both dogs were fastened to the pipes by heavy chains that rattled each time they moved. Although he knew that they could not reach beyond the full extension of their chains, Frankie was never fully convinced that he was safe from them.

Two stone steps and a low wide door in the far wall led up to a smaller kitchen, and beyond that was the gloomy pantry where trussed birds and enormous rounds of butter and cheese were stacked on cold stone slabs. Drums of powdered milk and dried egg were kept there, and sometimes the walls were hung with dead rabbits and the flagged floor littered with bloody skins.

The dogs began to growl as Frankie turned the knob of amber glass with both hands and pushed the door open. Sweetheart was sitting in her favourite chair with her legs crossed at the knee and a magazine spread out on the table before her. She turned the page with elegant fingers, seemingly unaware that Frankie had entered the room. She was counting: 'Nineteen. Twenty. Twenty-one.'

He crept into the kitchen and closed the door behind him, making sure its heavy curtain stretched right to the wall on either side. With both hands he smoothed and adjusted the long sausage-roll of cloth that hugged the bottom of the door to keep out those icy draughts ever present in the rest of the house. The room was stiflingly hot, and he was late.

'Twenty-two. Twenty-three.'

He climbed on to the high stool, acutely conscious of the heat of the stove and the growling dogs behind him. A plate pushed to the back of the table bore the remains of the Irishman's breakfast: little curls of bacon rind, stains of yellow yolk and the lacy brown edges of eggs fried to a crisp in the pan. There were tracks in the cooled fat where chunks of bread had been used to mop up the tasty juices of the meal. On a smaller plate set before Frankie was a sandwich made with thickly sliced bread, best butter and strawberry jam. It had been cut into four equal portions, two of which still bore the indentations of her fingers. The big cup with the chipped handle had been filled almost to its brim with milky cocoa. Its chocolate-scented steam rose to touch his nostrils, reminding him that he was very hungry.

'Twenty-four. Twenty-five.'

Frankie knew the drill. He stared straight ahead, hands clasped tightly in his lap, back straight, head up, shoulders squared. He must not look at her until she told him to do so. Nor must he scratch his head or allow his gaze to flicker, even momentarily, to the fleshy white mounds bulging over the slashed neckline of her blouse. Most of all, he must not look at the food on his plate. The smallest mistake could cost him his breakfast.

Perched uncomfortably on the high stool, he pressed his ankles together to prevent any movement of his dangling legs. He was aware of her pale hands with their long crimson fingernails, her fiery-red mouth and the coppery reflections of firelight in her hair. She drank from a cup so transparently delicate that its contents could be seen right through the patterned china. Her napkin was of pure silk with a neatly monogrammed corner. Her butter-knife had a shimmering pearl handle and a blade of polished silver. She frequently reminded him that she was a gracious lady fully entitled to beautiful possessions. She told him her perfume came all the way from Hollywood, in America, where she herself would have been living these last nine years if only Frankie's birth had not robbed her of the life of glamour and excitement she deserved. Now the heady scent of Californian Poppy filled the air and pushed the stale damp smell of the boy's unwashed clothes back against his body. He wanted to weep. She shamed him with her pale, clean, movie-star beauty.

'Twenty-five.' She repeated the words softly. Her breasts rose and fell in a deep sigh. She was always reluctant to punish him. She would not have the heart to do it, were it not for his own good. With her finger and thumb she plucked a quarter of the sandwich from his plate and threw it to the nearest dog.

'You dawdled,' she admonished in her gentle sympathetic voice. 'How many times do I have to tell you not to dawdle? Oh, how can a child of *mine* be so lazy and disobedient . . . so *ungrateful*?'

26

His eyes began to sting. He heard Lady whine her disappointment as the taller, quicker dog snapped another piece of Frankie's sandwich from the air and swallowed it in a single gulp. Sweetheart poured tea into her cup from a pretty tea-pot, adding milk from a tiny jug and sugar-cubes gripped in small silver tongs. Her lovely fingers merely hovered momentarily over the sugar-coated biscuits arranged on a china plate with tiny pink flowers and a fluted edge. At last she sighed heavily, closed her magazine and sat back in her chair with her hands clasped in her lap. She stared at him for a long time. He sat perfectly still, waiting.

'Oh, Frankie,' she said at last. 'When are you going to start growing? You're so *small*. Why must you be such a disappointment to me?'

'I don't know, Sweetheart. I'm sorry, Sweetheart.' He muttered the words unhappily. He hated to disappoint her. He had tried his very best to grow. He had even tried to stretch himself by hanging from the limb of a tree by his hands until the skin on his palms was blistered. Every muscle in his body had ached as if stretched to its limit, but it had not made a scrap of difference to his height. Someone once told him that horse manure in his wellington boots would make him grow taller, but the boys at school had made fun of him and Mr Sunderland, the headmaster, had called him a stupid gullible boy and made him scrape his boots and wash them clean in the outside drain and scrub his feet in hot water and carbolic soap. Some of the bigger boys still called him 'Little Shit-Legs' and held their noses when he came near. He did not want to be small. He was the smallest boy in the class and he prayed every night that God and His Angels would help him to grow.

'You're a dwarf, that's what you are.' She leaned forward to hiss the words in his ear. 'You'll grow up to be an ugly wizened little monster with short arms and a big head. No wonder your father hates you. You're a dwarf. What are you? *Say* it! What are you?'

Frankie swallowed his misery in a choking lump.

'I'm a dwarf, Sweetheart,' he mumbled.

'What? What are you?'

'A dwarf.'

'Say it again, *louder*!'

'I'm a dwarf . . . . I'm a . . . a . . . dwarf.'

He tried to sniff back the wetness that had sprung to his eyes, but a few hot tears managed to spill over and course down his burning cheeks. He flinched as Sweetheart lifted her hands in the air and let them fall back into her lap with a sigh of exasperation.

'You make me sick. Do you know that? Just look at you, whining like a baby. Oh, you make me so *sick*. Stop that snivelling and eat your breakfast, *dwarf*.'

She returned to the brightly coloured pages of her magazine, leaving Frankie to eat the last remaining quarter of his jam sandwich in peace. The room was silent save for the angry swishing sound she made each time she turned the magazine's pages. He sipped his cocoa and placed the empty cup on his plate. He did not know how to tell her that he was very, very sorry for being small, and for snivelling, and for ruining her life so that she could not go to America to be a film-star.

'Now get upstairs, *dwarf*. Get out of my sight.'

Frankie slid from the stool and walked towards the door on the prickly cushions of numbed feet. He could hardly believe that she was letting him go, that he was not to be punished for what he had witnessed in the best room in the middle of the night. The sharp hiss of an angry breath drawn through clenched teeth stopped him in his tracks. He was appalled when he realized his omission. Impossible as it seemed, he had forgotten that he must never, under any circumstances, leave her presence without kissing her cheek as a dutiful son should always do. He turned quickly, his eyes wide and anxious. She was seated in her chair like a cold stone statue, her face turned upward and away as an indication of her contempt. He took great care not to touch her or allow his grubby clothes to come into contact with her beautiful skirt and creamy-white blouse. After wiping the back of his hand across his mouth he stood on tip-toe and stretched up to brush her powdered sweet-smelling cheek with his lips. She accepted the kiss with icy disdain, and his misery was complete. Then the two dogs strained at their chains and snapped their teeth at him as he crossed to the door and quietly left the room.

He was stepping from the corridor's linoleum to the chilly tiles of the main hall when he spotted what appeared to be a golden opportunity to redeem himself. The enormous main door of the house stood open, its metal-lined bulk held by the largest safety-chain he had ever seen. When he peeped through the gap he could see the big half-pillars supporting the lintel, the rounded stone steps leading down to the paved walkway and the wilderness of garden beyond. He bent his legs in a squat and strained his head sideways in order to squeeze through the confined space without disturbing the safety-chain. A moment later he was outside in the bright morning sunshine. The front walkway was deserted, though he could hear the murmur of voices coming from the pigsties past the trees and bushes. He descended the nearest flight of steps to where bushes of peonies grew in untidy profusion, their blossoms well past their prime yet still magnificent. The first few he tried to pull free simply fell apart in his hands, scattering their petals like so much unwanted litter. He persevered with his task until he had succeeded in collecting an armful and pushing them, one by one, through the partly open front door. Back inside the

29

house he gathered them into an oversized bunch and headed for the kitchen, leaving a trail of fallen petals in his wake. She was still reading her magazine. She did not look up as he struggled to open the door and stepped inside, where he stood perfectly still, hardly daring to breathe for fear of dropping his awkwardly held gift.

'I thought I told you to get out of my sight.'

'Yes, Sweetheart, but I . . . I . . . .'

'You what? Stop that stammering and speak properly.'

'I . . . I . . . brought these for you.'

As she lifted her head to look at him, he proudly held the peonies at arm's length and prayed she would not notice their many imperfections. At that precise moment both dogs jumped against their chains and the fearsome Rosie began to bark. Frankie leaped to one side with a cry of alarm, jolting and almost dropping the bunch of flowers. The remaining petals fluttered to the floor in a pathetic cascade. In an instant his fine offering consisted of nothing but a tangle of leaves and twigs and the pale unlovely innards of dead blossoms. Mortified, he dropped his arms in a gesture of defeat, and the ruined peonies fell like garden rubbish around his feet.

Sweetheart stared at the mess on the kitchen floor, then at the unhappy little boy, then back at the ruined flowers. Slowly her features softened and her eyes began to twinkle with merriment. She tightened her lips against the chuckle that began as a small sound deep in her throat, but her amusement would not be contained and soon she was laughing loudly and helplessly. Stung by her mockery, Frankie hung his head and stared at the remnants of his intended peace-offering. There were tears in his eyes when he crouched to gather up the debris, scooping it into a pile with both hands while Sweetheart roared with laughter. She kicked a cardboard box in his direction, and he began piling the leaves and petals inside. Then he stood awkwardly beside the box, feeling utterly miserable, not knowing what to do next and so deeply humiliated that his face began to twitch. When Sweetheart spoke again, her voice had lost its caustic edge.

'Shall we go out to see a film tonight, Frankie? Just you and me? We could see Jane Russell again at the Empire, or walk up to the Arcadian to see *Sanders of the River*. I think it would be nice to see the Jane Russell film again, don't you, dear?'

Frankie nodded vigorously. He sneaked a glance at her from beneath his brows, his head still lowered. He allowed several moments to pass before daring to return her smile. Then his smile became a sheepish grin and his shoulders hunched in a giggle. Everything was all right. She was no longer angry, and he was not to be thrashed for spying on her and Tom Fish. He had succeeded in pleasing her in spite of everything that had happened. His gift of stolen peonies was discarded in a cardboard box, and she did not seem to mind at all. He had made her laugh. She was pleased with him. He was to be allowed to go to the cinema with her. For the moment at least, she had forgotten that he was a dwarf and the biggest disappointment of her life. She was still shaking her head from side to side and laughing softly when she shooed him from the kitchen and returned her attention to her magazine.

4

THE MAN IN THE ATTIC began to move about again around mid-morning. He aimed a noisy jet of urine into the metal bucket in the corner, then emptied phlegm from his throat in a series of growls. He began to cough in rasping barks that became horribly convulsive before eventually subsiding. Presently his feet took up the restless pacing that had become the rhythm of his curious existence behind the locked attic door. By now the sounds of his waking hours were familiar to the boy curled up in an army greatcoat in the room below.

Although Frankie had been dozing, he was too hungry to sleep for more than a few minutes at a time. He left his cocoon of warmth, closing the folds behind him so that the damp chill of the room would not invade his secret place during his absence. He crept from the room to the shadowed corridor, tip-toed past the attic door to the little corner where the banister curved into the wall. He knew he had not been dozing very long because the smells of fried bacon and toasted bread still drifted through the house. He guessed that she had not yet taken the man his breakfast. There was still time for Frankie, if he was very quiet and very careful, to eat his fill.

From that angle he could see the lower corridor running from the great square of the hall to the heavily curtained kitchen door. That area was dark and gloomy even in the daytime, with doors leading to permanently locked rooms, padlocked cupboards and deep curtained alcoves. Here, too, was the door to the cellar, that awful place dropping beneath the main staircase into the very bowels of the house. Glancing to his left, he wondered why the Bogeyman chose to live in a room on the first-floor landing instead of making his lair in the cellar, where he would surely feel more at home.

Crouched in the shadows at the curve of the banister, Frankie stared down at the dark jungle of coats and jackets hanging from a row of wall-hooks in the lower corridor. Below them was a collection of boots and shoes, gardening tools, cardboard boxes, books, cooking utensils, spare vehicle parts and horse leathers. A pair of wellington boots stood below a big black overcoat in such a way as to give the impression that a very tall man was standing against the wall, watchful and silent. Frankie had learned to be wary of that place. He knew how easy it was for someone to conceal himself amongst the clutter of hanging garments, unseen and unsuspected, while even grown-ups went about their business in ignorance of his presence. He could never pass along that section of the corridor in comfort. Whenever he stood at the turn of the great stairs, with the entrance-hall and main door at his back, he knew he was facing the very worst the house could offer. To his left the row of coats like so many black and patient predators; to his right the secret horrors trapped beyond the cellar door; and between them, at the very end of the unlit corridor, Sweetheart's daytime room, the kitchen.

Frankie shifted his position so that his knees would not become cramped. A smile tugged at his lips when he remembered the dead peonies falling at his feet and Sweetheart's totally unexpected laughter. He could not recall when last she had laughed at him without

33

ridicule. The times were few and far between when she could look at him and not be reminded of his many faults and shortcomings. However hard he tried, he somehow always failed to be the son she wanted; the son she truly deserved. Without doing anything at all he could make things happen for which he must be punished with slaps, missed meals or verbal assaults that left him trembling and incoherent. She might break a fingernail or drop a cup simply because he was present in the room. She might even return to the house after suffering a miserable day because of him. Her mood could escalate into a screaming rage almost without warning, and for that, too, he was responsible. There were times when his grandma or his aunties made trouble for him behind his back, or when someone would comment on his lack of height and Sweetheart would punish him for the embarrassment he caused her.

At other times he would come running in answer to her call to find her seated before the stove with her legs stretched out to the fire and her face softened by smiles. Then he would pick up the silver hair-brush and groom her hair in slow strokes from its dark roots to its glowing auburn ends. Or he might be handed a file and a tiny silver tool with which to clean her toenails while she dozed in a chair. He would sit or kneel until his body ached, picking and stroking in his efforts to please her. On very special nights he was allowed to stand beside her hot tub in a steamy bathroom heated by a small portable fire and smelling of sweet herbs. He would rub a soft soap-filled sponge over her back and shoulders, and his eyes would widen in wonder at the pure whiteness of her skin and the plump coarse rosebud teats jutting like angry things from her breasts. Against her creamy paleness his hand was a thin brown intruder, and he knew there were times when she despised him for his swarthy colouring.

Frankie stared through the banisters, willing the kitchen door to open. When she came with the tray he would slip downstairs and steal what he could from the open shelves in the pantry. Already his mouth was watering at the prospect of sinking his teeth into a thick slice of bread liberally spread with best butter and sprinkled with sugar from one of the big sacks standing in the corner.

While dozing he had dreamed, and in the dream he had seen Buddie brandishing his long-bladed knife and passing like an avenging angel through crowds of jostling raucous birds in the turkey-pen. He had been wearing his turned-down wellington boots and long rubber apron, and the gold in his teeth had flashed with reflected sunlight. Swinging his arm from left to right, he had scythed through one row of skinny necks after another until every bird was decapitated and motionless. Then the dream had shifted to show him whistling as he worked over the bins. He reached his hand inside each bird to strip its innards away before tossing the empty carcass on to a pile on the ground. Gradually one bin became filled to its brim with heads and feet, another with slippery, gaily coloured entrails. Then Buddie had slapped his thighs and bellowed with laughter as the biggest bin overturned and its slimy contents rushed towards Frankie in an oozing wave. The boy had woken from the dream with a start. It always made him sick when he was expected to watch the turkey-killings. Once he actually fainted in the mud and had to be carried back to the house and revived with cold water. Buddie had been very angry, but everyone else had laughed at Frankie and called him a snivelling cissy. Big Irish Tom had pulled down his shorts and grabbed his willy to show everyone that

35

he was truly a boy and not some soppy little girl who fainted at the sight of turkey innards. It had been a frightening and humiliating experience. More than that, it had served to prove yet again that Sweetheart was quite justified in calling him worthless and good-for-nothing.

Although Buddie seemed to loom like a lusty giant over Frankie, he was a good deal shorter than the other men who worked around Old Ashfield. He was even smaller in height than some of the women who came to the house. Black Blossom dared to tease him about his height and wiggle her huge breasts in his face to show how much taller she was by comparison. He was a squat muscular man with freckled brown skin, strong arms and dry sand-coloured palms that made rasping sounds when he rubbed them together. He had a habit of spitting into his hands and licking moisture on to his fingers while he worked. Buddie had travelled to every country in the world. On one of his more exotic voyages a skull and crossbones had been tattooed on his shoulder by a Greek sailor who used ordinary blue ink and a sharp pin to stab the design into the skin. Frankie liked the tattoo. It reminded him of pirates and buccaneers and fearless men who roamed the high seas in search of adventure.

Buddie always wore a hooped ear-ring in one ear and a chain around his neck decorated with the teeth of strange animals. Some were human teeth, big molars mounted by their biting edge so that the roots hung against his brown chest like deadly pincers. Gold tips flashed from his mouth each time he smiled, and his black hair curled in springy coils around his ears and neck. He was a quick noisy individual who laughed a great deal and sang or whistled constantly. He was also quick-tempered in a way that sent Frankie scuttling for cover whenever he raised his voice. He would ride the boy on his shoulders or shove him roughly aside according to his mood. Frankie never made the mistake of approaching him without invitation. Instead he shrank warily into the background until coaxed or ordered forward, and always took full advantage of those times when Buddie showed an interest in him. He looked forward to rare trips through the city in a dirty truck that stank of oil and pig-swill, the occasional shared chore, the songs, the rough companionship. He only wished he could grow taller and tougher and learn not to twitch and stammer with nervousness, that he could stop biting his nails and scratching his head so that his father would no longer hate him.

The kitchen door opened at last, and suddenly she was framed in its bright rectangle of light. She looked like a gypsy princess plucked from the pages of a storybook. Her blouse was scooped so low at the front that it left her shoulders and upper arms bare. Her waist was pinched by a broad black belt pulled tight by leather thongs. A full skirt of crimson and black swelled over her hips and was lifted and pinned at one side to reveal a cascade of lacy petticoats. She was wearing his favourite peep-toed shoes with ankle-straps and deep two-colour wedges. Her shoes came all the way from America, where such things were only worn by famous film-stars. Her ear-rings, too, were a gift from some exotic place. They jangled when she moved and brushed her creamy shoulders each time she turned her head.

The boy rose to his feet, still gripping the banisters and staring down at the figure in the doorway. He watched her drape a folded sheet and towel over one arm, then pick up a covered tea-tray and step from the bright kitchen to the gloomy corridor. He backed away, knowing he was invisible on the darkened landing yet fearful of the pale eyes that seemed to penetrate every shadow with their knowing stare. By the time she reached the shorter flight of stairs on the half-landing, Frankie had retreated all the way to his room and closed the door behind him, leaving only the smallest gap through which he peered with one eye. She was still smiling. When he could smell her perfume and hear the soft rustle of her skirts, he closed the door fully and held his breath. He heard the bolt slide from the attic door, then her tread on the stairs and the muffle of voices as she reached the upper room. He listened for some time before judging it safe to tiptoe downstairs. She would be occupied in the attic for some time. He must take his chance while the rest of the house was quiet. With half his attention on the attic and the other half on the Bogeyman's door, he slipped from his room and hurried downstairs.

His first priority was to climb on to the rim of the sink and peer through the upper left-hand corner of the kitchen window. From that position he could satisfy himself that the pig-swill truck was gone from its usual spot in the rear driveway. Then he took a slice of bread from the wooden board and, keeping as far away from the growling dogs as possible, crossed to the cooker in the far corner near the pantry door. The fat was still warm in the pan so that it soaked into the bread like water into a sponge. He turned the bread over to grease its upper side, then climbed on a stool to cut another thick wedge from the loaf. This he spread right to its crusty edges with butter from the huge round on the shelf. Then he unfastened one of the big sacks of sugar and pressed the bread, buttered side down, into the sweet white granules. He wrapped this and the fat-soaked bread in sheets of clean newspaper taken from the bathroom, then climbed back on to the stool to see what else he could find. He was lucky. There were plenty of crumbs to be gathered from around the cheese and scraps of meat and tasty skin to be picked from the carcass of a cooked chicken. Into his small cup he ladled a measure of fresh goat's milk from a jug on the window-ledge. Then he was ready to carry his stolen feast back to his room.

As he re-entered the main kitchen the dogs leaped to their feet, sniffing the air. On one of his recent trips they had frightened him so much that he dropped his food and had to watch helplessly while they devoured every last scrap of it. And once he had heard Sweetheart coming down the stairs, her high-heels ringing on the stone steps, and he had thrown the stolen food in Rosie's corner in a panic. It was gone in a trice, saving him from a terrible thrashing or many long hours standing in disgrace. Sweetheart hated thieves. She had once explained that slaughtering animals secretly and trading on the black market was simply bending the law a little and not really stealing at all, but real thieves were as bad as liars. They deserved to have their fingers chopped off.

A thick woollen blanket, charcoal grey with a band of dull red stitching across its upper and lower edges, formed a closely fitting blackout at his bedroom window. It was fastened with nails at its four corners to keep all daylight from the room. She told him it was there because of the air-raids in the war and even now, in 1951, there were special reasons why it must never be removed. Frankie freed one lower corner of the blanket and spread his sheet-music copy of *'Ain't Misbehavin'* across a section of the dusty window-ledge. He pulled the blanket around his back and hooked the frayed patch over the nail so that the light from the window would not be spotted if the door was opened. After wiping his hands very carefully on the tail of his grubby vest, he unwrapped the parcel and placed his food on the makeshift paper plate.

Upstairs in the attic, Sweetheart's laughter was a sound as pretty as music. Beyond the window, sunshine slanted through the trees to fall across Frankie's face as he enjoyed his morning feast. It looked like being a nice day after all.

5

LATE IN THE AFTERNOON Frankie found himself standing awkwardly by the kitchen door wearing polished shoes that pinched his toes and a shirt fastened at the neck with a large safety-pin. His trousers were properly creased and reached all the way to his ankles. They were real grown-up long trousers exactly like those worn by the boys at the big school. He had brushed most of the knots and tangles from his hair and scrubbed his skin until it hurt. He wanted to look his best so that Sweetheart would not be ashamed to be seen out with him. He had even threaded a length of wire flex though the tags in his waist-band to stop his trousers from slipping down over his hips whenever he put his hands into his pockets. Now he stood near the door with his hands clasping each other behind his back and his scalp itching furiously in the heat. His legs were beginning to get twitchy and fidgety, the way they always did when it was particularly important for him to keep them under control. The same thing always happened to him at school if he was brought out to the front of the hall for talking in assembly, or if he had to stand in the aisle with his hands on his head for not paying attention in class. He could never trust his legs, especially when his shoes pinched so badly that they made his feet tingle and twitch with pins and needles.

He had been standing in the kitchen for a long time. He guessed he was in disgrace again, because neither

Sweetheart nor Buddie had spoken to him since he was called down from his room almost an hour ago. They were both very angry, but they were silent now because the shouting had stopped, leaving a sharpness, an uncertainty in the atmosphere that Frankie could almost taste on the tip of his tongue. All that remained of the laughter of that morning was the cardboard box filled with dead peonies and shoved against the wall in the corner by the sink.

A boiled egg and two slices of buttered bread had been laid out at his place at the table. By now he was hungry again and anxious to eat while he had the opportunity, but he dare not move from the corner until told to do so. He flinched nervously as Buddie growled to gather phlegm into his throat, lifted the lid off the stove and spat on to the hot coals. Anger always made him do that. Frankie stared at the floor and tried not to think of all the things he might have done, or failed to do, to cause this latest upset.

It occurred to him that he had not worn his best clothes for many weeks; not since that confusing afternoon when some of Buddie's friends had rushed through the house carrying boxes, cases and sacks that must not be discovered when the police came to search the place. The man in the attic had been dragged through the gaps under the roof to one of the empty houses next door, and from there to the bushes down by the beck where the sound of his coughing would not give him away. The stuff about which they were all so concerned seemed to vanish into the most inaccessible shadows of the house. After a great deal of hunting around with flashlights, the plain-clothes policemen were forced to go away empty-handed. Frankie had been told to dress in a hurry, and Sweetheart had taken him to the park near the old railway bridge in Horton Park Avenue. Wearing his very best clothes and shoes, he had played all alone in the pouring rain while she and a balding detective discussed important business behind the steamy windows of a police car.

Frankie's twitchy legs and itchy scalp pulled his thoughts back to the present. He managed to shift his weight from one cramped uncomfortable foot to the other. The movement was slow and sly to avoid drawing attention to himself. He stole a furtive glance at Sweetheart. She was wearing a blue costume with a slit skirt that opened when she crossed her legs. The jacket had padded shoulders and a pinched waist, and its buttons were covered with glossy brown fur. She had pulled a pretty knitted skull-cap over her head and pinned it in place with metal grips. Her long hair was pulled through its centre to spring from her crown like a pony-tail that swished from side to side as she moved. In her ears were clips that matched the buttons on her costume jacket; rounds of soft brown fur lying darkly against her pale skin. As always, the scent of Californian Poppy wafted about her in perfumed clouds. Her legs were crossed at the knee, and she was wearing her new wedge-heeled shoes. He could tell she was very annoyed by the way she jogged her foot up and down as she stared at the window.

Buddie was still wearing his working clothes, though his big wellington boots with the turned-down tops were standing in the yard outside the kitchen door. His chair was pulled close to the stove so that he could prop one elbow against the chimney as he studied the pages of his newspaper. The dogs were quiet. Rosie cringed and showed the whites of her eyes when she looked up at her master. She was a big ill-tempered animal cowed by a presence more threatening and a temper more volatile than her own. Her pups were now piled together in a cardboard box lined with an old woollen jumper and several sheets of brown paper. The Great

Dane curled her long body into the remaining space and lay with her head resting on her front paws, oblivious to the pups' wails of hunger.

'Give him the damn jacket and stop being such a petty bitch.' Buddie spoke the words without looking up from his newspaper.

'I do not accept charity,' Sweetheart said coldly.

'Charity my arse. It's a gift from one of his aunts. She made it specially for him, and I'm damned if I'll send it back.'

'I want nothing from those people,' Sweetheart snapped. '*Nothing*. She only sent the jacket to spite me. I have my pride, you know. I don't see why I should be made to feel embarrassed just because your bloody sister wants to show off with her new sewing machine.'

'Don't be so damn selfish, woman. If you could be trusted to look after the kid properly, he wouldn't *need* clothes from other people, would he?'

'Have you even *looked* at it? It's the wrong size. It's far too big for him.' She sighed angrily, then narrowed her eyes into slits and stared at Buddie's broad back. 'And just *who* dares to say that I don't look after my son properly? What lies have your sisters been spreading about me this time? Answer me, damn you. I have a right to know what goes on behind my back.'

Buddie continued to stare at his newspaper. His silence made Sweetheart even more angry. Her face became twisted and not so pretty, and as her voice grew louder it lost its cultured tones and took on a snarling harshness.

'It's your bloody mother, isn't it? What has she been saying? That interfering old cow has never liked me. She's a liar, and you know how I hate liars. She makes up stories just to turn you against me. She hates me. She's *always* hated me. She's always trying to make trouble for me, because she's nothing but a jealous,

44

vindictive old woman. They're *all* jealous of me, *all* of them.'

Buddie lowered his newspaper and turned his head to look at her from beneath furrowed black brows. He stared into her pale furious face for a long time. He did not need to raise his voice or even explain that this was his final word on the matter. His tone alone was sufficient to convey as much when at last he said, slowly and very quietly: 'Give the kid his jacket, woman!'

Frankie tensed and lowered his head. He had known all along that it must be his fault. He was very sorry, but at the same time he could not help feeling excited by the prospect of owning a new jacket. He jumped sideways in sudden fright as Sweetheart snatched up a brown paper carrier-bag with looped string handles and flung it across the room. It struck his arm and fell to the floor, spilling out its dark contents. In the silence that followed, he cautiously stooped to pick it up, his eyes widening as the gift unfolded in his hands. He slid his arms into the sleeves and wriggled his shoulders until the stiffened collar stood up around his ears. He could scarcely believe his good fortune. Some-one had sent him a jacket almost exactly like the ones the famous bomber pilots all wore during the war. It was so dark a blue as to be almost black, with button-down cuffs and epaulettes and a broad welt that fastened around his hips with a buckle. Set into the side-seams were two deep slit pockets. One of them contained a silver sixpence which Frankie turned in his fingers but did not remove in case Sweetheart, in her present bad mood, took it away from him. Down the front of the jacket was a row of brass buttons similar to those on his precious army greatcoat, and on each breast was a pocket with two pleats and a pointed flap. He stroked his hands over the dark fabric and

45

shifted his shoulders against the silky lining. It was a wonderful jacket. It was thick and heavy and very large across his narrow shoulders, but it was the finest jacket Frankie had ever seen, and it belonged to *him*.

Buddie turned his head and looked at Frankie from beneath his scowl. He nodded without smiling.

'Go upstairs and take a look at yourself in the mirror,' he said.

Frankie left the room without daring to glance at Sweetheart again. He would not know what to do if her eyes told him to stay when Buddie had given him permission to leave. His toes were aching so much that he went upstairs very slowly, walking flat-footed to avoid bending his tingling ankles. On the gloomy half-landing he stared into the mildewed mirror. His reflection stared back at him with eyes that were big and dark in a small-boned face. Even in long trousers and polished shoes and a brand-new bomber jacket, he looked much younger than his nine years. He was different in other ways, too. He was not brown like Buddie, with crinkly hair and pale palms, but a certain swarthiness of the skin set him apart from all the other boys he knew. At school they called him 'Gypsy' or 'Mex' or 'Tie-Tie-Italiano'. He had learned to bear their ridicule without so much as a tear, but the names Sweetheart called him when she was really angry could make his body hurt like a bad pain on the inside. He prayed she was wrong, that he was not *really* a nigger, because niggers were coal-black people who lived in holes in the ground in darkest Africa. Their faces were like monkey faces, with thick lips and pointed teeth and ugly flat noses. Niggers ate children and ran around naked and plastered their skins with dog-dirt. Frankie could not be one of them, yet he feared in his heart that it might be true, because when

46

she called him 'Nigger' it wounded him in a special way he did not really understand.

The scrawny swarthy-skinned kid in the mirror blinked back at him. He raked his fingers through his hair and watched it spring back around his face in untidy tufts. He gave his scalp a good scratch, then smoothed his hair down as best he could and twisted the longer bits at the back into a coil which he stuffed inside his collar. Today it did not matter so much that he was different. Today he was wearing long trousers and a very remarkable jacket, and it did not even matter that his shoes were too small for his feet or that the safety-pin at his throat was digging into his flesh. He was luckier than all the kids in all the streets and all the schools in Bradford. He was going to the cinema for the second time that week, with his beautiful lady, his Sweetheart, who looked and smelt and sometimes spoke like the real-life star of a Hollywood movie.

'Time to go, Frankie.'

Her voice was warm again. As he hurried downstairs he heard Buddie leave the house and Lady the bulldog barking excitedly in the yard. Sweetheart was standing in the kitchen with a small satisfied smile on her face. She folded some pound notes together and pushed them inside her underslip, then looked over her shoulder to make sure that the seams of her stockings were straight. In the corner by the stove Rosie whined and pulled against her chain. While her back legs trampled the pups in the box, her gaze was fixed on the door through which Lady had passed to the freedom of the yard. If Rosie was released from her collar and chain, she would charge through the house and grounds like a homicidal maniac in search of something to destroy. She had recently killed some of Buddie's hens and turkeys by gripping their necks

47

between her teeth and shaking them violently from side to side before throwing them into the air. Buddie had beaten her with a stick until her mouth bled and she could barely stand. He had threatened to shoot her, and Frankie had dreamed of her blood-stained body dumped in the cellar with all the dead pigs.

Sweetheart's footsteps rang in the flagged yard. For a brief moment the boy was alone and unobserved in the hot kitchen. He made a dash for the table, snatched up the boiled egg and stuffed it into his pocket. By the time she reached the gate at the top of the yard, he was striding dutifully at his mother's heels. She turned right, taking the route that would be easiest and less damaging to her lovely new shoes.

The goats were tethered on a patch of grassy ground close to one of the gates. Frankie gave them a wide berth. He particularly hated the billy, with its ragged white beard and devil's eyes. The animal seemed to take a perverse delight in terrorizing him. It would pin him up against the nearest wall and try to eat his clothes, or chase him until his cries of fright attracted everyone's amused attention. He feared the goats only marginally less than the snorting, grinning pigs, and only then because the five nannies and their billy were usually safely tied up in the long grass.

'Come along, Frankie darling. You may hold my hand.'

Trotting after her, Frankie automatically rubbed his hand on his trousers before daring to reach for the gloved hand she offered. He looked up to see that she was smiling down at him in such a way that he could not help grinning in response. He felt his nose crease and his eyes screw up with pleasure. His shoulders lifted towards his ears as if to help the grin along. Her smile was like a shaft of warm sunshine falling across his face. It made him so excited that he had to cover his mouth with his free hand in order to stifle a ripple of laughter.

They walked together up the slope from the gate, passing the long high wall of Brooke Parker's chemical works and the wide opening that led to the top of Thorpe Street. They passed the big houses in Ashfield Place where all the doctors and veterinary surgeons lived, then made a left turn into Great Horton Road, which swept right down the hill to the town centre.

Frankie stared along tree-lined Ashgrove, where all the Americans stayed in specially converted houses with wind-up gramophones in every room. Its far end was crossed by busy Morley Street before continuing on to Lower Ashgrove, which led all the way to Grandma's house in Lansdowne Place.

Their path took them down beyond the Technical College and the School of Art building, where Buddie and two of his sisters posed as living models for the students. Sweetheart was going to be a model, too, but not until the school's principal found the good sense to send her maliciously jealous sisters-in-law packing. Although his aunts had always been kind to him, Frankie tried his best not to like them because he knew they were only *pretending* to be nice. He would be poisoned if he accepted food or sweets from them. Even their kisses might give him a disease from which he would die or become horribly spotty. Sweetheart knew about these things. She constantly needed to caution him about the many dangers he was either too young or too stupid to recognize for himself.

While they walked she explained to him that no other boy in the whole of England could even *hope* to own a bomber jacket like his. Whatever lies Buddie chose to tell about it, she and Frankie would tell everyone the truth: that it came in a big parcel from across the sea in America. It was a special gift from a

49

famous actor in California who had tried to persuade Sweetheart to join him on a luxury tour of Europe. She had declined the offer, of course. Because of Frankie she had graciously rejected the opportunity of a lifetime. Much as she deserved to travel the world with people of her own social standing, she could no longer hope to do so with a happy heart and a clear conscience. Never before had a mother been forced to sacrifice so much for her child. She could only hope he was grateful, and truly so, for all she was forced to suffer on his behalf.

Frankie *was* grateful. Indeed, there were times when his gratitude pressed down on him like a crushing burden slumped across his shoulders. He had ruined her life. Sometimes the terrible debt he owed her was a churning sickness in his stomach that often rushed into his throat to warn him that one day it might choke him to death. He knew that without Sweetheart's loving protection he would be put in a *Home* with criminals and perverts and mad people who attacked small boys. For his own good she frequently reminded him of the horrors and deprivations that would befall him there. Walking beside her now, he prayed she would not notice the peculiar tic that jerked his face into a spasm of nervous twitches and always made her so terribly angry.

6

THE EMPIRE THEATRE was a wonderful place. It stood at an angle behind the Alexandra Hotel near the bottom of Great Horton Road, tucked away on the curve of Randall Well Street. It was a cosy palace of velvet tip-up seats with brass ashtrays and little numbered plaques. Frankie knew every gilded swirl and cherub, every plaster rose, every painted bulb in each of the hanging light-fittings. He knew the smell that came from dust and stale cigarette-smoke, from shoes and overcoats and old stained carpets. The ceiling was painted a dark maroon, with tiny pin-points of light set here and there in the plaster to glow like stars in the night sky. And when the lights dimmed there was darkness of a different kind, friendly and safe. The Empire was a warm haven where Frankie could watch his favourite films or close his eyes and sleep without fear. High on the back wall was the window of the projection room, where strange machinery aimed its flickering beams at the big screen and by sheer magic produced talking, moving, living pictures. In this place he could find Roy Rogers, Gene Autry, the Lone Ranger and Tonto. Cartoon characters chased each other across the screen, glamorous women won the hearts of kings, innocent settlers set themselves against ruthless cattle-ranchers, war heroes plotted and schemed and died for their beloved country.

They sat downstairs in a double seat in the back row. They always chose an aisle seat so that Sweetheart could slip away to talk to her friends without disturbing anyone. She would stay until the first intermission, then leave him to watch the last complete performance alone. Sometimes Frankie would curl up in the big seat and sleep until she shook him awake shortly before the second feature came to an end. Tonight she was smiling as she stared up at the screen, and Buddie had given her money. If he was really lucky, she would leave him sixpence to buy ice-cream from the lady with the tray.

They had watched the film so many times that Frankie was familiar with every scene. Jane Russell bore a striking resemblance to Sweetheart. She had the same smouldering eyes and pouting lips, the same tiny waist and big swelling breasts. When Sweetheart fixed her hair and make-up a certain way and dressed up in the clothes she made on her treadle sewing machine, she looked for all the world like Jane Russell come to life from the big screen.

She had a marvellous memory. She could play the heroine's scenes from a score of films or recite long passages from the Holy Bible that she had learned as a child. Sometimes, when she was all alone in the house, she would call Frankie downstairs to sit with her in the kitchen by the fire. Even the dogs would be hushed as she told the story of the highwayman who came riding, riding by, or the shipwrecked sailor lost in a terrible storm, or the faithful lady who died by the gun to warn her lover that he was riding into a Roundhead trap. She conjured wonderful colourful pictures for a boy to see with his mind's eye, her voice pure and confident, her memory pouring out hundreds of lines of poetry in a faultless, almost hypnotic flow.

Frankie glanced up to see her quietly mouthing the words as lights from the screen flickered across her face. She was so clever. Other boys' mothers had rough

52

hands and plain faces and knew nothing except cleaning and cooking. They lived in poor houses with
outside lavatories, and their clothes stank with the oil
of the woollen mills or the dankness of unaired ward-
robes. They were all bitterly jealous of Sweetheart
because she was so clean, with beautiful hands, long
painted nails and a face like a film-star's. And she
knew absolutely *everything*, which must have made
her particularly disappointed in Frankie's slow progress at school. His reading was hesitant owing to a
stammer that tied his tongue whenever he was
expected to give account of himself before the rest of
the class. His handwriting was so bad that Mr Sunderland had pinned his composition to the notice-board in
the hall so everyone could see he was the worst writer
in the whole school. He was baffled by arithmetic and
hopelessly confused by those twin horrors, history and
geography. They called him a dunce at school, yet he
knew all the words of the records on Sweetheart's
wind-up gramophone, and every song Buddie's friends
played when they got together with their instruments
in the big downstairs room. He had learned the steps of
all the dances and the names of the singers. He could
even identify the more famous musicians by their
individual styles. He knew Duke Ellington, Errol
Garner and Louis Armstrong, and singers such as Fats
Waller, Ella Fitzgerald, Nellie Lutcher, Vera Lynn,
Bing Crosby and a dozen others. He knew them all, but
somehow his special talents always failed to impress
those who really mattered. He could also ride a horse,
with or without a saddle, and hit a target ten times out
of ten with arrows from his bow, but neither of these
things seemed to count. He was still the school dunce.

Sweetheart sighed heavily as the final credits faded
and the lights brightened to reveal only a handful of
patrons dotted around the cinema. She propped her

handbag in her lap, took out a small mirror and carefully smoothed the swept-up sides of her hair. With her little finger she flicked melted lipstick from the corners of her mouth, then dabbed at her nose and cheeks with a small powder-puff. Finally, she gave her head a shake that set her ear-rings dancing and her pony-tail skimming across the back of her seat. Frankie knew she was preparing to leave. When the lights dimmed again she would slip out by the rear exit, and it would be dark outside and very late when she came back. One night she brought him to see a horror film about the Living Dead, and he was so frightened by the zombies that he fled into the foyer in a panic. He had expected her to be sitting in the little ticket office with her friend Maureen, but instead he found the office locked and in darkness and the entire frontage of the cinema deserted. Unable to return to his seat, too scared even to hide in the toilets, he had hovered in the shadows by the door for a long time until he spotted Sweetheart climbing from a car parked on the other side of the street. Then he had dashed back inside and curled up in his seat with his hands covering his ears until she came to take him home.

Tonight there would be no such frights. The B film was a Western starring Randolph Scott, and when that was over he would watch Jane Russell again, and somewhere in between he would eat his boiled egg and perhaps sleep for a while.

From the loudspeakers on the corner pillars came a selection of popular songs by Gracie Fields. People began filling up the empty seats. Many were wearing their Sunday best, the ladies in hats or newly pressed headscarves, the gents in overcoats and polished shoes. Most of them went through the ritual of gazing about them with curious eyes in search of a familiar face among the crowds. Sweetheart appeared oblivious to

54

their stares, but Frankie knew she was aware of all the eyes that turned in her direction as she sat with her legs crossed and her head lifted proudly. Several courting couples pushed their way along the back rows to cuddle close together in the deep double seats. There were few children lucky enough to visit the cinema mid-week, as he so often did, and that made Frankie feel particularly privileged.

The ice-cream lady with the curly brown hair walked slowly up the aisle, her head turning this way and that in search of last-minute customers. The lights began to dim, and the big gold curtains swished back on their noisy invisible pulleys. Sweetheart reached up to touch the ice-cream lady's arm. Their heads bent close together, and whispered words were exchanged. Coins rattled in the tray's money-compartment, then Frankie felt his hands close around the chilly wrapping of a choc-ice. He stammered his thanks as the Western sprang to life on the screen and Sweetheart slipped from her seat in a waft of perfume. His heart sank the way it always did when she left him. By now he was used to spending longer and longer periods alone, yet in that moment when she walked away he always experienced a brief sense of loss that made him want to rush after her and beg her not to go. Moments later the parting was forgotten as Randolph Scott, flanked by a posse of brave volunteer deputies, galloped across the screen in search of the notorious Bodine Brothers from Kentucky.

Frankie woke with a start. Someone was shaking him by the shoulder as the band played 'God Save the King' and everyone else in the cinema stood to attention. He scrambled to his feet, knuckling sleep from his eyes with both fists. He must have fallen asleep during the Jane Russell film. Now the main lights were on, the ruffled gold curtains closed across the screen, the exit doors wedged open. It was almost ten o'clock. Tonight he must face the very thing he had always dreaded. The show was over, and Sweetheart had not come back for him.

He stood on the bottom step long after the heavy metal grids had been pulled across the foyer and the last of the cinema lights turned off. It was dark and cold, and he was completely alone. He heard the Town Hall clock chime the hour and he could not ignore the growing fear that this time the very worst had happened. She had left him, just as she so often threatened to do. There were mill-owners in Bradford and Leeds who had been begging her for years to leave Old Ashfield and go to live with them in their fine houses. She had spoken of a rich businessman in London and a gentleman farmer in Sussex, both of whom were madly in love with her. Any one of them might have taken her away. A woman like Sweetheart could have any man she chose, so long as she was willing to leave her son behind.

'Well, well, well, if it isn't young Frankie from Old Ashfield.'

He started nervously and sniffed back a tear. He had been too engrossed in the anguish of his own thoughts to notice the approach of the two uniformed policemen. They came via the narrow snicket leading past the Alexandra Hotel into Great Horton Road. He wondered if they had come to take him away to a *Home* for ungrateful and unwanted children. They stopped close to the step where he was standing. One of them looked at his wristwatch, pursed his lips and scowled fiercely. The other was a stout man with a dark moustache. He winked an eye at his companion and said to Frankie: 'Been to the pictures, have we, son?'

Frankie nodded and sniffed again. The frowning

56

policeman bent down to stare into his face. His breath smelt of cigarette-smoke and peppermint.

'Where's your mam, Frankie?'

'She'll be back soon . . . er . . . in a minute . . .,' he stammered.

The policeman with the moustache stood erect with his hands on his hips. He was grinning now. He winked again and nudged the other man's arm.

'Gone to have a little chat with a friend, has she, son?'

'Er . . . yes . . . I think so.'

'Been gone long, has she?'

'No . . . no . . . not very long.'

'Left you in the Empire all by yourself for a couple of hours, I suppose. Looks to me like she's forgotten to come back for you, son. 'Appen she had better things to do, eh, George?'

Both men guffawed at the remark, while Frankie looked from one grinning face to the other. He was embarrassed. He felt that they were making fun of him, though he could not understand why. He knew that Buddie hated all detectives and uniformed policemen. These two seemed friendly enough, but their questions about Sweetheart put him on the defensive. She had always told him never, under any circumstances, to let other people know their private business. He must tell them nothing. Even if they locked him in a dark cell and pulled out all his teeth with rusty pliers, he must keep his promise to Sweetheart and tell them nothing. His heart leaped and his knees trembled with relief when he heard the unmistakable sound of her footsteps rounding the corner at the other side of the cinema building.

'Frankie! Oh, Frankie!' Her voice was high and anxious as she rushed towards him. 'Oh, *there* you are,

57

you naughty boy. How many times has Mummy told you not to wander off like that?' She caught him up in a breathless embrace, then gave a little gasp of alarm as she seemed to notice the two policemen for the first time. 'Oh dear. Good evening, officers. I do hope my son has not been making a nuisance of himself.'

The two men grinned broadly and shook their heads.

'We were just a bit concerned that he was left on his own so late at night.'

'Oh, but he *wasn't* left alone, were you, Frankie darling?'

Feeling sick with relief that she had not run away with a rich man, Frankie shook his head vigorously in agreement and clung to her arm. She laughed prettily and tossed her head, her eyes flashing with amusement.

'One moment we were all sitting outside the Art School discussing the latest models, and the next moment the boy had wandered off by himself. Isn't that so, Frankie darling? I don't mind telling you, I've been almost *frantic* with worry this last half-hour. I can't *imagine* what his father would say if he found out about this. My husband has such a *terrible* temper. He'd probably take a belt to the poor boy.' She completed her speech with a deep sigh and an extra hug for Frankie. He wanted to weep.

'I'm sure there's no need to worry yourself about that, missus.' The policeman with the moustache was still grinning. 'Look, George, why don't you walk the boy on ahead while I have a private word with his mother?'

Sweetheart smiled and released Frankie into the care of the other man, who gripped him by the shoulder and looked terribly stern.

'Go ahead, dear,' she insisted. 'Mummy won't be a moment.'

Frankie went reluctantly, straining his neck in order

to keep her in his sight. He watched her throw back her head and laugh at something the policeman said, then move very close to him as he wrote something down in his book. A few minutes later she hurried back and took him by the hand. As they walked up towards the main road, he was surprised to see her turn round to wave at the policemen as if they were old friends.

When they reached the main road she pulled him roughly across to where Irish Tom's van was parked. He was bundled into the back among the old tyres and coils of rope, while she climbed into the front beside the driver. After a very bumpy ride they alighted at the top of Thorpe Street and the Irishman drove away. Sweetheart gripped his hand and they hurried in silence down the side of Brooke Parker's and through the iron gate at the bottom of the slope. The lamp outside the turkey-house was still burning to illuminate their way along the front drive and into the yard. She paused briefly to tidy her hair and smooth the creases from her skirt, then led the way into the house.

Buddie was sitting on a hard chair with one foot resting on an upturned petrol-tin. His back was bent over his guitar, his lower lip sucked in and his brows furrowed in concentration. He glanced at the clock and nodded his approval without breaking the rhythm created by his fingers on the strings. In spite of everything, they had managed to reach home at their usual time.

'Bedtime, Frankie.'

Sweetheart's voice was soft, relaxed. She stooped rather stiffly to offer the boy her cheek. He kissed it with lips wiped dry and germ-free on the sleeve of his jacket. Buddie caught his eye and nodded. Still painfully relieved that he was not to be made an unwanted orphan and bundled off to a *Home*, Frankie left the room without a word. He stopped outside the bathroom to remove his shoes and massage the cramps from his toes. Later he paused at the top of the shorter flight of steps until he was sure it was safe to pass the Bogeyman's door, then tip-toed along the corridor to his room.

Curled up in his army greatcoat, Frankie listened to the snores of the man in the attic and hoped and prayed that neither Sweetheart nor the two policemen would tell Buddie that he had wandered off and become lost. He dreaded the feel of the big leather belt across his bare legs and buttocks. Almost as frightening was the bellow of Buddie's voice when it grew huge and powerful with anger, and the shouted words that struck like blows to make Frankie flinch and tremble. His own imagination offered a punishment far in excess of his crime. He knew he was guilty, because Sweetheart told him so. He was almost afraid to fall asleep in case he was pulled from his bed in the middle of the night and thrashed.

7

'AS OF TODAY, you must *not* call me "Sweetheart".'

The boy looked up from his porridge, his spoon poised in mid-air and his face solemn. He was well aware of the importance of a new name. He knew he must pay particular attention if he was to avoid the consequences of using the wrong name, especially in public. She continued to buff her newly varnished nails, smiling a little to herself. She was wearing something pink and pretty that covered her body in soft folds. For a moment he entertained the hope that he might be allowed to call her 'Mam', the way he used to, or even 'Mummy', as she always called herself when speaking to other people. He was disappointed.

'My name is "Smallfry",' she announced. 'From now on, you will only call me "Smallfry".'

Frankie nodded obediently and stared down at his porridge. He had heard the name before, in a song recorded by Bing Crosby. One of the musicians who played in the band with Buddie had once ruffled Frankie's thick black hair and called him 'Smallfry' in a way that was not meant to be unkind. He had liked it. It was a nice friendly name for an adult to give a child. There was nothing wrong with the name, but it would embarrass Frankie, so small and thin for his age, to call his own mother 'Smallfry'. The boys at school were sure to snigger at him behind his back, and the Irishman and his rough friends would have one more excuse to belittle him for their own amusement.

'Let me hear you say it,' she said, her voice cutting into his thoughts.

'*Small . . . fry.*' He pronounced it as two separate words, very deliberately.

'Again. Say it again.'

'Smallfry,' he repeated, and the name sounded ridiculous to his ears. He had wanted so much to call her 'Mam'.

She smiled and extended both arms to examine her manicure in detail. When she tossed her head her hair fell around her shoulders and upper arms in a lovely auburn cascade. Frankie liked her hair. He enjoyed brushing it, even when she made him stand so long behind her chair that his arms ached and his eyelids started to droop. He was always happy to help her keep her hair beautiful, even when it was time to use the greenish-brown powder that reminded him of warm cow-dung when she mixed it with water. She called it *graduated henna*. It came from one of the huge stone jars in the herbalist's shop near the bottom of Manchester Road. The man in the light-brown coat spooned the henna powder on to fancy scales with tiny brass weights, then folded it into a sheet of brown paper tied up with string. The gloomy cluttered shop always smelt of black spanish and hot blackcurrant juice and strong bitter-sweet sarsaparilla. Sometimes Sweetheart had to go into the back room to buy something special. Then Frankie was left perched on one of the high oak stools, staring at ranks of miniature wooden drawers with unreadable labels. He liked to sniff the parcel of *graduated henna* for its strong herby smell. When mixed with warm water the powder became a dense paste which Frankie plastered all over her hair. He worked from the root, soaking strand after strand until her whole head was covered in the gritty concoction. When no trace of hair remained visible, he applied strips of newspaper and a warmed towel to complete the process. Much later, it was his job to rinse her bowed head with bucket after bucket of warm water until her hair was scrupulously clean once again. He liked the smell of her shampoo and the way it foamed into a soft white froth between his fingers. Sometimes he even managed to keep for himself the little piece of cotton-wool that she soaked in perfume so that he could rub the henna stains from her skin. After the treatment her hair shone like burnished copper from scalp to tip, such a beautiful shade of red that people turned in the street to stare as she passed by.

'Are you listening to me?'

He jerked his senses back to the present with a start.

'Yes, Sweetheart.'

'What? *What* did you call me?'

'Smallfry ... I meant to say Smallfry ....' He dropped his gaze from her face to his empty bowl. 'I'm sorry ... Smallfry ....'

He heard her sigh deeply, the way she always did when he let her down in some way. The two dogs were whining softly in the back of their throats and sniffing the air as if distressed. Their food was boiling in a pan on the back burner of the gas-stove in the alcove by the pantry door. The smell of the steaming meat tormented them until their mouths slavered and their eyes rolled. It bubbled and spat through a layer of brown scum that stained the outside of the pan, but it smelt good, almost as good as the dinners Frankie sometimes had at school. There was left-over porridge in the smaller pan. He could see it steaming where it coated the rim and the long-handled wooden spoon. Although he was still hungry, he decided against asking her for second helpings now that he had forgotten to use her new name at the very first test. Instead he glanced at her delicate china tea-cup and saucer and marvelled afresh that he had never, in all his life, actually seen her eat.

On Thursday morning the nurse from the clinic arrived at St Andrew's. She was there to examine the children's heads and bodies for lice, injury, infection or disease. Her visits were a cause for much speculation and a great deal of dread because her power was infinite. In a single school term she had once sent to private sanatoriums as many as four boys and two girls with a weakness of the lungs. As many more were ordered to their homes with notes declaring the presence of head-lice. One girl's facial impetigo had to be painted with ointment that stung the scabs and branded her with unsightly violet-coloured splotches for several weeks. Almost a third of the pupils were obliged to eat worm-cakes and do their busy on sheets of newspaper until someone from the clinic was satisfied that they were no longer a threat to the health of fellow-pupils. Frankie had been one of those unfortunates. The nauseating taste of the worm-cakes and the humiliation of the treatment were only outweighed by the sheer relief of being freed from an incessant itching in his backside. Worms were horrible things. They lived inside a person's body and wriggled about until their presence drove him to distraction.

Now the nurse from the clinic was visiting the school again, and Frankie was the only boy in his class who had failed to return his slip of paper duly signed by a parent or guardian. He told his teacher he had lost it on the way to school, and Mr Watson promptly rapped his knuckles with a ruler for his carelessness.

Nurse was a thin woman with a lined face and watery blue eyes. Her hair was twisted into tight steel-grey rolls on which sat her clinic cap with its distinctive badge. Her hands were cold, dry and unfriendly. She examined little boys as if they were made of much sterner stuff than mere flesh and bone. She pinched ears, lips and nostrils, pulled hair and poked her hard fingers into tender places, and she did so with a vexed expression on her face, as if the worried children in her charge deserved to be roughly handled.

The boys queued in sets of five outside the headmaster's room, each clutching his signed slip and praying he would not be singled out for special treatment. Frankie had scrubbed his hands and feet and dampened his hair with water to make it lie flat and tidy against his head. He told himself that the itching in his scalp was just a heat rash, and determined not to scratch his head in the presence of the nurse. He did not want to let Smallfry down again.

Nurse smelt of toothpaste and disinfectant, and crackled when she moved because her clothes were so stiffly starched. Her shoes squeaked on the polished linoleum. She exuded power: the power to change a boy's destiny with a stern shake of her head and only a few official-sounding words. Her antiseptic presence transformed Mr Sunderland's office into a place where children were condemned not to the cane or detention but to threadworms or impetigo or a terrible weakness of the chest that could only be treated in some distant sanatorium.

Frankie had nits in his head. Nurse found them and cracked them between her fingernails the way Smallfry sometimes did when he was made to kneel with his head in her lap, breathing her perfume and savouring the rare closeness of her. Nurse found the worst patches around his ears where he had scratched the scalp sore. She discovered the dirt and thickened wax deep in his ears, the grubbiness at the back of his neck, the hoof-like skin on the soles of his feet, the bitten nails. She examined Frankie from head to toe with prying eyes and searching, penetrating fingers; and she found him lacking.

He was sent home at lunch-time. He had brought no money, so he was not allowed to join the untidy crocodile of children forming the dinner queue. On the opposite side of the corridor were the free-dinner kids, those embarrassed boys and girls who enjoyed a daily privilege for which others were forced to pay. Frankie often joined his classmates in taunting them because of their poor homes or absent fathers, yet in his heart of hearts he envied them all. To be a free-dinner kid was to enjoy a full stomach every single day of the week, puddings and all.

By fumbling around in his desk until the others had lined up for dinners, Frankie managed to avoid the harsher ridicule of those in his class who were free of head-lice. With Nurse's letter folded in his hand, he ran all the way down to the infants' school on the corner before stopping to catch his breath. On the other side of the road the cobbled slopes of West Brook Place rushed down to the walled beck before the land swept up again, steep and thickly wooded, to the terraces of Old Ashfield. If he squinted his eyes, he could just make out the greyness of the roof between the trees and here and there the stony finger of a chimney-stack. He knew he should turn right into Longside Lane, then left down the long hill that was Shearbridge Road, then left again and up to the very top of Thorpe Street. At this time the men of Brooke Parker's would be loading their wagons with the globular bottles that Buddie called *carboys*. Fashioned from smoky green glass, tightly corked and wired, they would be packed with straw for protection and carried on wooden poles slotted through their individual baskets of woven metal. Frankie liked to watch the loading. When the factory doors were open, Brooke Parker's became a fascinating place of acrid steam, acid-like smells and grim-faced men in protective aprons.

Frankie hesitated. It was a long way home via Shearbridge Road. If he took the short cut across the beck, he would arrive there in a fraction of the time. The letter in his hand aroused in him a sense of urgency that offset his fear of the narrow enclosed footpath known locally as Dead Man's Alley. Alongside and beneath the alley, Mucky Beck rushed for half a mile past walled mill-ponds, wasteland and cinder piles all the way from Shearbridge Road to Cheshum Street. He knew that this tunnel-like place was shunned by tramps and feared even by drunks and peg-sellers. Mucky Beck was a frightening rat-infested torrent, with steep moss-stained steps at either end of the alley and untold danger lurking in the shadows between.

Frankie's palms were already sticky with perspiration when he crossed the road, ran down West Brook Place and squeezed through a gap in the high brick wall at its lower end. Here the alley stretched to both left and right in gloomy curves. He could hear the beck-water rushing beneath the flags at his feet. He could see the grassy wilderness forming a high bank beyond the old bulging stone wall that held back the encroaching hillside. The branches of trees stretched out as if to peer over mill walls or rest themselves against the windowless rear walls of factory buildings. They formed a canopy that robbed the area of light. It was an eerie place, full of strange sounds and dank smells and things too frightful for a small boy to contemplate.

Frankie hesitated, his heart pounding against his ribs and his mouth suddenly dry. He had entered Dead Man's Alley at its halfway point. He was not sure if he should tip-toe slowly and cautiously along until he reached the lower grounds of Old Ashfield, or make a sudden dash for it in the hope of outrunning any danger that might be waiting to pounce. Smallfry had told him that a body had recently been dumped at the tunnel entrance where the beck came into view for several yards before vanishing again into the darkness below ground. It was the body of a young woman. She had been brutally assaulted and strangled, her body mutilated and her throat slashed from ear to ear. Council workmen checking for land subsidence found the horrible remains close to the tunnel's mouth and ran off in a panic to raise the alarm with their screams. The killer was still at large, and the activities of hungry rats, as well as the most terrible injuries, meant that the body had never been identified.

Thoughts of butchers' knives and bloodied axes galvanized the boy into frantic action, but he had no sooner broken into a sprint along the alley than the sound of his own footsteps stopped him in his tracks. He was wearing the leather shoes that had been only for best until they grew too small for his feet and now had to be worn for school. They pinched his toes and rubbed the back of his heels and made a *rat-tat* sound on the stone flags that echoed through the spooky quiet to announce his presence. He pushed Nurse's letter into the pocket of his pants and glanced nervously about him. Then he sat down on the ground and quickly removed his shoes and socks. He could run and jump and climb much better in bare feet, and he could do it all without making a sound. For a moment he paused to massage the circulation back into his tightly compressed toes, then he was racing along the narrow alley as fast as his legs would carry him. He ran with the blood pounding in his ears and the words of a half-forgotten rhyme spurring him on:

'Up the airy mountain, down the rushy glen
We dare not go a-hunting for fear of little men.'

He ran without daring to look back. Walls of red brick rose up on his left like sheer cliffs. Walls of ancient stone with the hillside at their backs pressed in on his right; smaller and less sheer but still impossible for him to climb. Then the alley curved sharply, first one way and then the other, and it seemed to Frankie that he would be trapped in that sinister place for ever. Just as he began to fear that he was running for his life through a nightmare landscape that had no end, the ground suddenly opened to reveal the rushing waters of the beck and the section of crumbling stone wall on its other side. Up ahead was the tunnel mouth and the outlet-pipe that carried waste down the hillside from the house.

At this point fear was his undoing. Without pausing to measure the distance, he launched himself into a desperate leap that carried him right across the opening. His bare feet connected with the smooth slime-covered surface of the conduit and slid away in different directions. With a shoe clutched in each hand he was unable to make a grab for the rougher stones that might have saved him from disaster. He toppled sideways with his arms flailing. An expression of pure horror shaped itself on his features as he slithered helplessly down the slope and plunged headlong into the stinking waters of Mucky Beck.

8

THE OUTLET-PIPE saved him. He managed to grab it
with both hands as the force of the water, aided by his
frantic struggles, propelled him into the yawning
mouth of the tunnel. He saw his own feet thrashing the
water like dying fish, and his good leather shoes
turning idly in the current as they rushed underground. Spitting and spluttering, he braced his body
across the pipe and clutched with both hands at everything within reach. The wall close to the tunnel had
crumbled, undermined by long years of dampness and
pressure from protruding tree-roots. Clumps of sturdy
weed grew wherever they could take a firm hold. It was
to these that Frankie clung as he inched his way
upward, making tortuously slow progress away from
the slippery edges of the beck. At last he succeeded in
hauling himself over the boundary wall to the solid
ground that marked the edge of Old Ashfield property.
There he collapsed in an exhausted heap, all strength
drained from his limbs. He was coughing violently, his
stomach heaving against the foul taste of beck-water.
He tried to wipe the wetness from his mouth using the
back of his hand, only to find his face smeared afresh
with a foamy slime. He spat the stuff from his lips,
then began the long difficult scramble up the hillside,
hauling himself from tree to tree by clinging to the
network of roots growing above ground.

At the top of the hill he rested. Nearby was the giant
oak where Buddie had tied a heavy rope, knotted at its

70

end, as a Tarzan swing for Frankie. Two of the bigger boys from Thorpe Street had once tried to outswing him for a dare, but Barry Lock had turned chicken at the last minute and Valance Fraser, who fancied himself as the cock of the street, had managed only a partial swing that left him dangling by his arms in the dirt. Frankie was an expert. He hoisted the rope to the very top of the hill, leaped into space with his bare feet wedged against the big knot and soared like an eagle over the tree tops. At its farthest point, that spot where he hovered high in the air before the rope changed direction, he knew that he was suspended sixty feet above Mucky Beck and the perimeter wall. The danger of killing himself in a fall was very real, but this was a fear he had learned to master, even to enjoy. It was the *unseen*, the *quiet menace* that defeated him.

He got to his feet and looked round. He had reached the flatter section of land at the side of the house where vegetables had once grown in neatly fenced patches. Towards the centre of that area were roses and rhodo-dendrons that had been left to grow like weeds, and a willow tree whose branches reached right to the ground to create a shady den around its trunk. Beyond the willow and the blackberry hedges was an untidy collection of huts and tin-roofed chicken-pens that Buddie had erected against the far wall. As always, the big wooden gate in the distance was locked.

Frankie walked towards the front of Old Ashfield. Overgrown hedges with concealed segments of barbed wire divided the hillside from the terraced gardens, so the front walkway could only be reached via its small wrought-iron gate. From there the long straight path-way of decorative crazy paving led past the houses to a matching gate at the far end. Beyond that, and hidden by a wide area of trees and bushes, was the group of squat brick houses where the pigs were kept. Smallfry

71

often spoke of Old Ashfield as a huge and stylish mansion built by a millionaire mill-owner at the turn of the century. The man had enclosed his fine acres, including the steep hillside and the land where the slag-heap now stood, in high stone walls to keep the common people out. Years later it was divided into three houses to accommodate a growing family, and now the middle house and its crumbling neighbours belonged to Smallfry and Buddie. While other boys lived in cramped homes built back-to-back in cobbled streets, Frankie had his very own room in a mill-owner's mansion too grand for common folk.

He was barely inside the terrace gate when he heard the dog. Barking ferociously, the big Great Dane rushed from the rear of the house, skidded around the corner and hurled herself at the gate with such force that it creaked under the impact. Frankie backed away as the animal's snarling head and powerful front legs hooked themselves over the top of the gate and her back legs struggled for a foot-hold on the curves of wrought iron. He knew from past experience that she was capable of leaping over to the terrace. She barked in frustration. Her black eyes were bright, her lips curled back in a fearsome snarl that dribbled saliva and left her tongue hanging. As she dropped to the ground in a crouch, preparing to make another attempt at the obstacle, Frankie turned on his heels and raced for the house. He heard Rosie scale the gate and gallop in pursuit. She was bearing down on him like a bull in full charge when he jumped the wide steps and with a cry of terror threw himself against the front door of the house. It jerked against the safety-chain, leaving a narrow gap through which he scrambled to safety. He was followed by a head and a paw as the now enraged Rosie attempted to squeeze herself through the same opening. Frankie scuttled away on all fours, his wet body skidding on the cold tiles and his breath coming in frightened little gasps. Moments later the furious barks and snarls became howls of pain as Buddie's wellington boot connected with the dog's jaw. Frankie got to his feet with difficulty. He felt sick. His knees were wobbling as if they might collapse under the strain of holding his body upright. In the gloom of the hall, Buddie sniffed and curled his lip in distaste.

'What the hell happened to you, boy?'

'The beck . . . the . . . the beck . . . . '

'And just what were you doing down there when you should be in school? Come on, boy, speak up. Stand up straight and stop that bloody twitching.'

Frankie lifted his head and stiffened his knees in an effort to prevent them trembling. His eyes blinked violently in a spasm that screwed up his face in rapid jerks. When he tried to swallow the lump in his throat he found that it tasted of beck-water. His words came out in a stammer.

'I had no d-dinner money . . . Teacher s-sent me home . . . Nurse said . . . she said . . . she g-gave me a note . . . . ' He fumbled in the pocket of his pants, withdrew the saturated letter and stared at it in dismay.

'Where are your shoes and socks?' his father demanded.

'The t-tunnel . . . dropped . . . I . . . f-fell . . . . '

Buddie's face suddenly loomed over him, distorted and shimmering in the poor light. The boy's knees buckled and the air left his lungs in a small sigh. He was aware of nothing more until he opened his eyes some time later to find himself lying naked on a sheet of tarpaulin in the backyard.

The long tin bath that usually hung by one of its handles on the wall of the pantry had been placed on the level paving stones at the bottom end of the back yard. A rubber hose-pipe snaked across the yard

73

from the kitchen window, bringing hot water from the tap in the big sink. The tin bath was half-filled with hot water into which had been poured the same perfumed green oil that Smallfry always added to her bath. Buddie worked in grim silence. First he scrubbed the boy from head to toe, using a piece of towelling and a bar of carbolic soap. Then he hosed him down with warm water until all traces of the beck had been removed. He smiled without humour when Frankie sucked at the soap-filled cloth in order to sluice the taste of rancid beck-water from his mouth.

He was sitting at the kitchen table, wearing one of Buddie's shirts and sipping cocoa from a large cup, when his nanny, Buddie's mam, arrived at the house. His hair had been cut very short but only shaved around his ears and towards the back of his neck. He was grateful for that. The boys at school who had to have their heads shaved because of nits were always fair game for the rest of the school. They suffered the kind of cruel teasing that drew them together, regardless of past differences, into closely knit little groups sharing a common stigma. Frankie could imagine only one thing worse than being counted amongst the 'baldies'. He had always dreaded being singled out as the *only* boy in the school with nits, a solitary outcast with a shaved head.

His nanny had a cure for nits. She plastered his head with a yellow liquid that stung like salt when it ran into his eyes. Then she gave him a fine-toothed comb that would drag the dead lice and their eggs from his hair after the liquid had done its work. A second application in two weeks, followed by another more careful combing, would completely rid him of the pests. The comb was made of shiny steel and it was his to keep. He determined to hide it away in his special tin

74

and only use it on Sundays, and in secret, to keep his head free of the nits.

Nanny was humming softly to herself when she took one of the big tins from the shelf to make a meal of corned-beef slices and wedges of onion fried in batter. Then she sat at the big table with only a pot of tea for herself while Frankie and his father cleared their plates in silence. At last she set down her cup and looked pointedly at the clock on the kitchen wall.

'Well?' she asked. 'Where is she?'

Buddie scowled. 'Leave it alone, Ma,' he said.

'Huh!' Nanny huffed the way she always did when she was annoyed at something. 'I would have thought it was a perfectly reasonable question. He might have been drowned, or savaged by that stupid animal.'

'I've told you before, Ma, not in front of the boy.'

His scowl had deepened, and there was a note of warning his voice. Frankie held his breath. An argument was about to begin. There would be trouble now, and it was all because of him. He looked at his nanny with desperation in his eyes. She patted his hand and smiled, then pursed her lips together as if they must be forced not to speak another word. For a while there was silence around the big table.

Frankie's clothes had been hung to dry over the hot-water pipes at the side of the stove. He saw Rosie stretch up, catch the damp pants between her teeth and slowly draw them down to her grimy sacking, intent on ripping them to shreds. Nanny saw it, too. She rose from her seat and swiped the dog a hefty blow across its snout. Frankie giggled. He liked his nanny. He wanted to forget that she was sly and spiteful and malicious. Smallfry said that she was a wicked old woman who pretended to be nice just to trick people into liking her and believing her lies. She accused

Nanny of making up stories about her and saying bad things to get Frankie into trouble. Smallfry hated liars. He must always believe the things she told him about other people, especially those in his father's family, but Frankie sometimes found her instructions very hard to understand. Nanny was good to him. She often did things and said things that made him feel loved.

Nanny lived in a big house on the corner of Lansdowne Place, near the club and the post office and opposite the big church. It was a boarding-house where foreigners and theatrical folk lived in upstairs rooms and the kitchens always smelt of stew and roasting meat, currant buns and freshly baked bread. It was a very noisy place. People sang or played musical instruments at all times of the day and night. Sometimes they cleared all the furniture back against the walls so that they could practise their special dance routines, or held rowdy parties in each other's rooms. They sat on staircases to talk about poetry or politics, and many of them smoked long thin cigarettes rolled in dark brown paper and smelling of perfume. Smallfry said the house was a hostel for whores and niggers and criminals on the run from the police. She hated Nanny. She called her a tart and a slut because she used to be married to a black man from South Carolina who sang basso at charity concerts all over Yorkshire and Lancashire and dropped dead at the Sun Hotel in Eccleshill in 1927. All their children, including Buddie, were born with brown skin and crinkly hair and grew up to be entertainers, just like their father. Nanny Fanny was also a Jewess, which caused a lot of bad feeling because Smallfry called herself a Catholic and so they believed in different parts of the Bible and were supposed to go to church on different days of the week. Frankie did not understand how it could be so important which end of the Bible they preferred to read or which church they were both too busy to attend every Saturday and Sunday.

Frankie had often spoken to one of the *very* black men who lived at Nanny's house in Lansdowne Place. He was a tall handsome man with huge white teeth; a magician who could conjure coins or playing-cards from inside the pockets and behind the ears of small boys. He said his name was Christmas and he had worked his magic act in theatres and royal palaces all over the world. He came from Ethiopia, and his skin was the colour of glistening wet coal except for the palms of his hands, which were sandy pale, and the whites of his eyes, which twinkled like sunshine on fresh clean snow. There were some dancers from Morocco in two of the first-floor rooms and a lady on the top floor who had once sung in an opera-house in Paris, France. Frankie liked Nanny's house because it was warm and brightly lit, but he was rarely allowed to go there alone because Smallfry knew things about it that he would never understand.

His other nanny lived in a small house on Park Road, close to St Luke's Hospital and not far from the park where Frankie sometimes played. She was Smallfry's mam, but she never, ever came to visit them at Old Ashfield. Her house smelt of beer and coal-tar soap, and the water in her taps was always hot. In front of the fire she kept a dark tab rug that she had made herself from scraps of different-coloured material. It was here that Frankie hid the black sharp-tasting seeds that he picked from her caraway cake. This nanny worked in the big brewery down Manchester Road, capping the bottles and loading them into wooden crates. She wore men's trousers under a wrap-around overall, heavy clogs on her feet and a scarf tied round her head like a turban to keep her hair in place. Yeast from the beer

beer in the brewery had caused a scaly rash to grow on her forearms and across the backs of her hands. The scales were dry and silver, and fell like little clouds of snow when she had to scratch the skin because the cream from her doctor would not stop the itching. She kept a pretty green budgerigar called Peter, who once dropped dead in his cage but came back to life when Nanny gave him a few drops of gin squeezed from a wad of cotton-wool. She was very, very fond of her budgie. She held it on her finger and sang to it and made little kissing noises with her lips that he tried to imitate. She made Frankie smile because she believed the bird could say all sorts of real words, when in fact it did nothing but whistle and chirrup and squawk.

His thoughts were brought back to the present when Nanny Fanny gave him a sandwich of buttered bread thickly spread with strawberry jam. She was watching him so intently as he bit into it that he began to wonder if Smallfry was right to fear she would poison him at the slightest opportunity. On the rare occasions when he went with Buddie to the house in Lansdowne Place, he must always say he was not hungry and refuse any food she offered him, just in case it was poisoned. He was often overcome with temptation when faced with such delights as chicken dumplings and ice-cream and treacle suet pudding, and so far he had been lucky. He had not died or fallen ill, nor had Smallfry been made aware of his lapses. Smallfry wanted to safeguard him against danger and jealousy. She could only do that if he kept her secrets and obeyed her instructions to the letter. Now he stared from the partly eaten jam sandwich to the homely face of his grandmother and wondered if she would dare to murder him in his own home with Buddie sitting right there at the same table. Nanny smiled. It made her face crease all over and her dark eyes twinkle. She was looking at him the way his other nanny looked at her budgie. She had a pleasant untidy face and chubby warm hands that were nice to touch. He knew he ought to be afraid of her, yet he found himself returning her smile with an easy grin and enjoying his jam sandwich to the very last crumb.

9

'COME OVER HERE, Frankie. I want you to touch Rosie's
head.'

The boy froze. Buddie was sitting by the fire. He had
picked up one of the pups and examined it roughly
before replacing it in the cardboard box with the
others. Frankie had hovered in the background, eager
to cuddle the puppy but not daring to approach the
bigger dogs. Now he shrank inside as a wave of
apprehension swept over him. He glanced at his nanny
for support. She was stitching the holes Rosie had
managed to rip in the seat of his pants in the few
seconds they were in her possession. She clicked her
tongue and shook her head but did not look up from
her work when Buddie spoke again.

'I said, come over here, boy. It's time you learned
how to be around Rosie without making her mad.' He
extended his arm and snapped his fingers impatiently.
'Do as you're told. Come here.'

Motionless on his stool, Frankie stared first at
Buddie's dark profile, then at the huge brown and
black body curled in the corner. She was watching
him. He could see the longer teeth at the sides of her
mouth and the folds of wet black skin that at any
moment would draw back in a threatening snarl. His
heart began to pound against his ribs, and his hands
trembled. He could not touch Rosie. She would tear
him to pieces. She would bite off all his fingers and eat
them, the way Smallfry said she would if ever he was

caught stealing. With Buddie's orders ringing in his ears, he stood his ground and made not the slightest move to obey. Although he feared his father's anger, he was unable to summon the courage to move closer to where the dogs were tied.

Buddie suddenly reached behind him with one hand, grabbed Frankie by the sleeve and yanked him from his seat at the table. The stool on which the boy had been sitting tipped over and hit the floor with a loud crash. Rosie immediately leapt to her feet, growling.

'*Down*,' Buddie said. 'Get *down*, girl. Take it easy. Come on, Frankie, touch her head.'

'No . . . I can't . . . .'

Frankie pulled back against the hand that gripped him. He felt himself yanked across the room and flung across his father's legs, his body protected while his outstretched hand dangled like bait in the dog's face. He struggled and pleaded, curling his exposed fingers into a fist that strained against the bigger, stronger fingers encircling his wrist.

'No . . . p-please, Buddie . . . no . . . .'

'Don't be a bloody coward, boy. She won't bite you.'

'She will . . . she will . . . .'

'No, she won't. Not while I'm here. Just keep still and don't let her think you're scared. *Quiet*. Get *down*, Rosie. Come on, Frankie. That's it. Let her sniff your hand.'

'No . . . n-no, Buddie . . . no . . . .'

'Stop snivelling. *Quiet*, Rosie.'

'No . . . no . . . no . . . .'

'Touch the bloody dog, damn you.'

'No . . . Nanny . . . Nanny . . . Nanny . . . .'

'Oh, for heaven's sake . . . .'

Suddenly exasperated, Buddie raised his free hand and brought it down in a resounding slap on the boy's buttocks. Frankie screamed. The heavy bulldog threw itself against its chain, barking and snapping. The Great Dane barked once and sank her teeth into the boy's dangling hand. Frankie screamed again. With a roar of rage, Buddie leaped from his chair, kicked the bulldog, struck Rosie a back-handed blow and shoved Frankie aside all in the same movement. Released at last, the boy scuttled crab-wise across the room, his injured hand hugged to his chest as a double row of livid bruises began to form on his skin. He scrambled to his feet and made a dash for the door, skidding to a halt only inches short of the now frantic bulldog. In the bedlam of yelling and barking he danced from one foot to the other in a brief breathless panic. Then he turned and flung himself into his nanny's arms.

The uproar in the kitchen continued for some time while Nanny pressed his face against her coat and added her own voice to the tumult. His injured hand was hot and throbbing. He could hear Buddie yelling at the top of his voice as he thrashed the dogs, and the rattle of chains as Rosie and Lady leaped about, barking and snarling in confused excitement.

'It's time you got rid of that lunatic Great Dane,' Nanny shouted above the din. 'Get rid of her before she does some *real* damage.'

'Mind your own damn business, woman,' Buddie yelled back.

'Look at your son's hand. *Look* at it.'

In her anger she grabbed Frankie's wrist and thrust out his hand so violently that his arm jarred against his shoulder and sent a searing pain through his upper body. The boy was too shocked and frightened to speak. Smallfry always threatened to lock him in the tool-shed with Rosie if ever he dared tell her secrets to anyone else. Now he knew that nobody, not even Buddie, would be able to save him from Rosie's deadly teeth. As he had always suspected, she was just waiting

82

and watching for an opportunity to rip him to pieces. His fear of the big dog suddenly increased beyond any fear he had ever known.

At last Buddie managed to beat the protesting Rosie into submission. She cringed in her corner, whining and docile. Lady followed her example rather than suffer at the hands of her infuriated master. Buddie snatched up Frankie's hand, prodded the swelling and squeezed the purple bruises in his search for a break in the skin. Then he kneaded the small hand in his big fists, searching for broken bones. Fright and the pain of the examination dried Frankie's mouth, turned his legs to jelly and clouded his vision.

'That was your own damn stupid fault,' Buddie told him. 'Why the hell must you always make a fuss? Why do you panic like a silly girl every time something scares you? Rosie only bites you because you make her so nervous. And stop that damn blinking and twitching when I'm talking to you, boy. *Stop it*.'

He raised his hand as if to strike Frankie, who instinctively recoiled into the rough safety of his nanny's overcoat.

'Leave the boy alone,' Nanny snapped. 'Save your rotten temper tantrums for those who deserve them. You can't blame Frankie for what happened. It was all *your* fault, you bloody idiot. You shouldn't have done that to him. No wonder he twitches. Between you and the dogs and that stupid bitch you're married to, he's frightened to death most of the time.'

'Watch your tongue, woman. Don't you dare slander my wife.'

'Slander? *Slander*? It would be easier to slander the Devil himself.'

'Cut it out, Ma. I'm warning you . . . '

Frankie wriggled free so that he could remove himself from the confrontation. They were cross with each other because of him, and now Nanny was saying bad things about Smallfry that would make Buddie very, very angry. Just then he saw a familiar shape pass the window on its way to the rear door, heard the tap-tapping of high-heeled shoes on the flags outside. The door in the corner opened, and Smallfry swept into the room wearing a glossy black costume with white fur trims and decorated combs in her hair. She dismissed Frankie with a withering stare that warned him to remain silent.

'What's going on?' she demanded. Her eyes narrowed into hostile slits as she met the cold gaze of her mother-in-law. 'And what is that woman doing in my home?'

'Taking care of your son while you're out gallivant-ing, as usual,' Nanny replied. She folded her arms across her stout chest and pursed her lips. 'Well? And just where was *Madam* when little Frankie was sent home from school?'

Smallfry peeled off her gloves and moved slowly and elegantly across the kitchen. She smoothed her hair with both hands, peering at her reflection in the mirror near the sink. She seemed totally unconcerned by the crackling tension in the atmosphere.

'Well?' Nanny demanded. 'Well?' She turned to Buddie and tightened her lips into a thin angry line. 'Ask her. Go on, ask her where she's been all after-noon, dressed up like a tart and missing for bloody hours. She does *nothing*. Look at this place. It's filthy. Why can't you make her stay at home like any *decent* wife and mother?'

'Now, you keep out of this, Ma,' Buddie warned.

'Like hell I will. I want to know where she's been and what she's been doing.'

Smallfry turned from the mirror with a brilliant smile. Her gaze swept over her mother-in-law from head to toe and back again, and her expression was one of open contempt. 'Where I go in my free time is none of your business, you interfering old cow.'

'What? Did you hear what she called me? I will not be spoken to like that . . . . '

'Then get back to your own house and stop pushing your nose in where it isn't wanted,' Smallfry hissed. 'Go to your room, Frankie.'

He jumped nervously at the sound of his own name. Buddie had taken out his little silver tin and was in the process of rolling one of those thin straggly cigarettes that flared when lit and vanished after only a few puffs. Nanny's face had changed colour, and her eyes bulged. She looked as if she might explode at any moment. Smallfry was smiling sweetly as she reached for Frankie's sleeve and eased him in the direction of the door. Beneath the fabric of his borrowed shirt, her fingers trapped and twisted his skin in a burning pinch that told him she intended to deal with him later. The instant she released him, he turned on his heels and fled.

On the small landing at the top of the main staircase he stopped to examine his reflection in the mirror. Light from the bathroom filled the area with pale shadows and gave the damaged patches in the mirror an eerie silvery glow. Dressed in his father's shirt, his mop of black hair savagely pruned and his skin scrubbed and glowing, he looked like a thin bewildered stranger trapped within the glass. He cradled his injured left hand in his right palm. He could feel the hotness of inflamed flesh and the steady throbbing of a dozen tooth-sized bruises. His father's smell seemed to be impregnated in the large cotton shirt that covered him from neck to calf. It bore no traces of pig-swill or motor oil or animal hair. It was the man's own smell, and Frankie would have recognized it anywhere.

He moved away from the mirror, seated himself a little way from the top of the main staircase and wrapped the tails of the shirt around his legs. It was cold on the stairs. Even in summer, when the grounds and gardens were so warm that Frankie could lie stark naked in the long grass, the house was dark and uncomfortably cold, especially on the big stairs. He leaned on the banister. He was sitting directly above the cellar door, close enough to the kitchen door to hear their angry words. By now Smallfry was using her other voice, the one that screeched shrilly and somehow managed to transform her from a beautiful movie-star into something savage and frightening. Nanny was also shouting. He could tell she was upset by the words she used: bad words he had often heard from the men who worked with the pigs or came to the house to drink with Buddie in the music-room. Even the dogs were quiet while the heated quarrel raged around them. Frankie heard his name mentioned several times and knew he would be punished when the row was over. It was all his fault. If only he had not caught nits and been sent home from school, fallen in the beck, lost his shoes, been attacked by Rosie or injured his hand just because he was too cowardly to follow Buddie's instructions.

'How *dare* you accuse me of neglecting my son.' Smallfry's voice rose to a scream. 'You foul-mouthed, trouble-making old witch. How *dare* you spread such vicious lies.'

'That's enough,' Buddie bellowed. 'That's *enough*.'

'You're a tart,' Nanny yelled. 'And you're a spineless little shit, Buddie, if you can't see what's going on and keep your own wife under control. That little boy is neglected, and all you care about is seeing Madam, here, dressed up in all her bloody finery.'

'My son is *not* neglected. We have a book full of

expensive photographs to *prove* how loved and well cared for he is. You're a liar, old woman, a bloody *liar*.'

Frankie nodded his head in the dim light on the stairs. He could not understand why Nanny was suddenly bent on making the worst kind of trouble for him. Neglected children were taken away and locked up in *Homes* where they were made to eat worms. Smallfry had told him so. Neglected children were sent to special schools and never allowed to see their mothers or fathers or nannies again for the rest of their lives. It must be true that Nanny was a liar and a trouble-maker because he could hear her saying all those terrible things that might cause Frankie to be taken away for ever. It made him feel better when he heard Smallfry mention the book, the special album in which they kept all the photographs of him wearing his best clothes and doing nice things. There was a big picture of him dressed in a fancy cowboy suit and Stetson hat, riding the pony Buddie had bought from a circus because it wouldn't allow the big men to ride on its back. There were lots of smaller snapshots of him sitting astride Trigger, or propped on cushions behind the steering-wheel of Buddie's truck, or standing in the garden in his very smartest clothes. He could also be seen riding on Buddie's back with a shiny red apple in each hand, and again walking beside Smallfry on the day she wore the big yellow roses in her hair. The pictures were proof that Frankie was not neglected. He was not certain of the exact meaning of the word, but he knew without doubt that it could not possibly be applied to him. The photographs in the album were absolute proof of that.

He leaped to his feet as the kitchen door suddenly opened, then crept backwards until he was concealed in the darker shadows beyond the turn of the banister. Smallfry looked up into the darkness. She was smiling

87

again, as if all the unpleasantness in the kitchen had meant nothing to her.

'Frankie darling, would you like to come downstairs and say goodbye to your grandmother?'

He recognized the tone of her voice and the particular expression on her face. Her hair looked very red in the bright light from the kitchen, and her ear-rings twinkled each time she moved her head. She seemed to stare directly into his face as he crouched in the shadows on the half-landing. He knew that smile. It told him not to move.

'Come along now, Frankie. Don't you love your grandmother enough to come downstairs and give her a little goodbye kiss?'

Frankie chewed his lower lip and frowned. He would never dare openly to disobey Smallfry, but he had learned to listen for every shift in her voice-tone and read for himself the most subtle variation in her smile. She was asking him to come downstairs. She was also telling him to stay where he was. As she turned away with a heavy sigh, he heard her say, almost sadly: 'The boy knows his own mind. I can hardly *force* him to kiss his grandmother when he so obviously doesn't wish to.'

The back door closed with a slam, and Frankie guessed that Nanny had left the house. He wondered why she had turned against him after cooking him such a nice meal and being so kind to him while Smallfry was away. Taking the oddly shaped metal comb from the pocket of his shirt, he ran it through the short oily hair on top of his head. He waited on the cold landing for a long time, nursing his throbbing hand, anticipating the moment when he must face his parents and the serious punishment that was surely due to him.

10

IT WAS LATE IN THE EVENING when she called him
downstairs. By then he was standing behind the blackout blanket in his room, a comic spread out on the
window-ledge where remnants of fading sunshine fell
in brassy yellow stains. Because the room was so cold
he had pulled on his bomber jacket over his father's
shirt. On his feet were a pair of odd socks that were
holed at the toes. His door was partly open. Even as he
studied the pages of his comic, his ears and senses were
alert to the smallest sounds coming from the rest of the
house. He would know in an instant if the Bogeyman
made a move, or if anyone left the kitchen by the
doorway into the hall. At the first sign of activity on
the ground floor, he pulled off his jacket and socks, hid
them in a corner and positioned himself at the bedroom door, ready to make a dash for the kitchen. He
was downstairs before she could call his name a second
time.

She had placed the worm-cake on one of her prettiest
saucers. It covered the space in its centre where the cup
was meant to sit: a thick ugly thing against the delicate
pink and white porcelain. Half the size of his palm, the
worm-cake was made of bitter chocolate whose only
hint of sweetness was in the sparse sprinkling of sugar
on its surface. Mixed with the chocolate was a horrible-
tasting substance designed to purge the impurities
from a boy's body by wringing out his insides in
dreadful spasms. He recognized Nurse's letter lying

89

amongst the litter on the sideboard. Someone had dried it out, unfolded and smoothed it until it resembled a sheet of grubby brown parchment. Nurse had said nothing to him about worms. He did not know if she had written it down in the letter, or if the cake was to be his punishment for all the bad things he had done. Already his stomach heaved at the prospect of swallowing and digesting the hateful thing.

A long time ago, Frankie had tried to give one of the worm-cakes to Rosie while Smallfry's back was turned. The big dog had snapped it from his fingers eagerly enough, but after rolling it around in her mouth a few times she spat it to the floor and pawed at it, growling and sniffing her distaste. Infuriated by what she called the actions of a wicked little sneak, Smallfry had forced him to eat every last crumb of the cake without allowing him to clean the dirt and animal saliva from its surface. He had feared he might choke when she stuffed chunks of it into his mouth and held him down, her hand sealing his lips, until he swallowed. Only her own determination had prevented him from vomiting it back. He had gagged for hours following the ordeal, convinced that one of the dog's hairs had lodged itself at the very back of his throat where his fingers were unable to reach.

Now he sat at the kitchen table with the worm-cake before him and the taste of nausea already on his tongue. He glanced at her out of the corner of his eye, wondering if he dare ask for water to help wash the cake down. She was sitting before a mirror that was propped against a large pan on the stove. Her hair was newly brushed and hanging loose around her shoulders. In the heat of the kitchen she had removed her costume jacket and hung it over the back of a nearby chair. Now she was wearing only a tight white brassière above her skirt. It seemed almost too small to contain the swelling plumpness of her upper body. It crushed and lifted her breasts to create the deep fleshy cleavage he always tried so hard not to stare into. In the gap between the brassière and the pinched waistband of her skirt, her flesh bulged in a pale soft band. From time to time she dipped her fingertips into a glass jar and withdrew them laden with cream which she smoothed into her face and neck in lazy strokes. Still peering from the corner of his eye, Frankie stared at her breasts for a long time before he realized with a jolt that she was observing him through the mirror. He snatched up the worm-cake and bit into it, forcing the bitter chocolate past the awful gagging in his throat.

He was struggling with his second mouthful when Buddie came to his assistance. The man burst into the kitchen carrying a great mound of kindling which he dumped in a pile by the door. He hung his heavy axe and rubber-handled flashlight on nails hammered into the edge of a high shelf, then shrugged his jacket from his shoulders and left it to lie where it fell. His boots hit the linoleum close to the door with a clatter. Although both dogs had grown quiet and drowsy in the stuffy room, they immediately struggled to their feet with a rattle of chains and a whined greeting. Even when the noise of his entry had subsided, his very presence seemed to alter the atmosphere in the room in some way. At the sink he filled a cup with cold water, drank it down in one gulp, refilled it and handed it to Frankie without comment. He lifted the boy's hand into his rough dry palm and poked at the pattern of bruises on both sides, scowling as he prodded each mark in turn. The skin was discoloured and quite swollen, but the burning sensation had eased and his whole hand no longer throbbed with the same intense pain. The boy looked up into his father's dark glowering face and tried his best to smile. He felt his efforts

91

twisted into a grimace by the soreness in his hand and the awful taste of the worm-cake in his mouth.

'You shouldn't be sitting around only half-dressed. Not in front of the boy.'

Buddie kicked an upright chair into a more suitable position and reached for his guitar. Carefully, almost lovingly, he pulled the instrument across his knees and began to pluck at the strings with a plectrum fashioned from tortoise-shell. It made a sweet clear sound in the quiet room. He seemed not to notice that his comment had met with no response. Smallfry paid him no attention. Instead she lifted her hair with both hands, smoothing it up from the nape of her neck and piling it on top of her head in a soft copper mound. The movement brought her breasts into clearer view, pushing them upwards and outwards against the restrictions of her tight brassière. Stealing a furtive glance into the mirror, Frankie was shocked to see another face, another pair of eyes in the glass. He looked quickly at the window behind his father's back and spotted Tom Fish outside in the yard. The grinning Irishman caught his eye, raised one massive fist in a threatening gesture, then pressed his finger to his lips for silence. Frankie felt his face redden and his cheeks begin to burn all the way up to his scalp. Smallfry continued to pose before the mirror, smiling and pouting her lips in film-star kisses to the man in the yard while Buddie picked out an intricate melody on his guitar. Trapped like a guilty thing between them, Frankie lowered his head and took another bite from his worm-cake.

She had given him some newspaper torn into squares and a glass of dark-brown liquid that tasted like spanish water. He had managed to fall asleep in spite of the lingering taste of the worm-cake in his mouth. It was pitch-dark and the house was very quiet when the first effects of the treatment woke him. He found his belly seething and bubbling with movements he could feel quite clearly beneath his hands. Then the griping pains started, and soon he was running along the unlit landing in desperate need of the lavatory. After countless such visits he was afraid to look into the bowl in case something of himself had been lost in his body's writhing struggles to empty itself. Pain and nausea swept over him in waves that left him hot and sticky and weak at the knees. For a while he thought he must be dying, that his nanny had managed to poison him after all. He could see his reflection, turned gaunt and ashen, in the fragment of mirror propped against the lavatory window. The lamp outside in the yard bathed him in grey light, leaving his eyes in deep shadow so that his face resembled that of a corpse. It reminded him of the zombies he had seen in the horror film at the Empire. The sight of his own face scared him. On several occasions he left the bathroom feeling weak and drained, only to stop on the dark landing at the onset of another wave of nausea. Then, clutching his belly with both hands and sucking his buttocks tightly together, he made one more panic-stricken dash for the little cubicle.

His squares of newspaper were soon used up. Exhausted, he sat down on one of the steps leading from the bathroom and leaned his brow against the cool wall. He had returned his father's shirt and now wore his own vest, washed in the tin bath and dried over the kitchen pipes. Even in that scant garment he was very hot and sweaty. He knew he would have to go in search of extra newspaper before the pains came again, but first he must rest and regain his strength after his exertions in the bathroom.

He was staring into the black well of the stairs when

93

he heard the noises. They were soft scratchings or shufflings, like the sounds made by an animal as it sniffed about in search of food. Something was moving around in the darkness. The hairs on the back of his neck suddenly prickled and stood on end. The noises were coming from behind the dark brown door on the first-floor landing. The Bogeyman was awake.

Frankie started towards the shorter flight of steps leading to the landing. He intended to make a dash for his room and wedge a broken chair-leg under the door to keep the monster out. Smallfry had forgotten to warn him because he had done so many bad things and caused a lot of trouble. Either by accident or as punishment for his sins, she had left him to the mercy of the Bogeyman.

The turn of a key in the lock of the brown door stopped him in his tracks. There was no time for him to get up the steps and past the door before it opened and deadly talons reached for him in the darkness. With a choked little cry he jumped backwards, turned and plunged into the unseen, gripping the banister and screwing his eyes tightly closed as he ran. He swung himself around the turn at the bottom of the stairs and raced blindly along the lower corridor. He reached the kitchen door just as a bright rectangle of light slowly spread across the upstairs wall. The sound of slow labouring footsteps could be heard moving along the first-floor landing as the boy threw himself into the kitchen and slammed the door behind him.

The room was faintly illuminated by the glow from the night-burning stove. Rosie's shadow loomed monstrously across the ceiling as she lumbered to her feet with a threatening growl. The bulldog twitched and sniffed the air, started to rise but thought better of it and flopped down with her head on her paws. The snorting sounds coming from her flattened nose were a half-hearted warning to the boy. In the other alcove Rosie barked once. She was straining against her chain with her lips curled over her teeth and her ears pinned back. It seemed to Frankie that she and her shadow filled the entire room.

He knew he was safe so long as he remained in the kitchen. Smallfry had told him so. The Bogeyman would never dare enter the kitchen. He edged his way to the gap between the gas-cooker and the wall, located the stack of newspapers and pulled a full one from underneath so that nobody would notice the pile had been disturbed. Then he ventured into the middle kitchen where most of the food was kept. He was not hungry. His stomach rebelled at the mere thought of food, but he knew he must not miss this golden opportunity to put something by for another day. He was looking for the bowl of eggs he had seen earlier. A small window on to the yard offered sufficient light for him to make out the cheese and butter and sacks of sugar and rice. He moved into the farthest room, which had a tiny square of window set in its far wall and overlooking the rear driveway. It was a small dark place with a dank smell, the coolest of the three rooms and often used for stacking the carcasses of rabbits, chickens and turkeys. Frankie groped around on the shelves until his fingers encountered a deep plate. He reached in with both hands, only to shrink back in horror when he encountered something cold and clammy beneath his hand. The plate contained pigs' trotters. His stomach heaved as he wiped his fingers down his vest. Pigs' trotters made him sick. They would be cooked into a greasy stew with vegetables and served up looking exactly as they did when they were raw: pale and nauseatingly realistic, with the toes and claws intact. He would be forced to eat what was placed before him because pigs' trotters were good for him and would help him to grow.

95

The lamp outside in the yard suddenly went out, plunging the dimly lit rooms into total darkness. Through the tiny back window Frankie saw shadows moving along the rear drive. There were men out there, workmen driving animals and carrying torches whose beams were aimed at the ground. Frankie forgot the eggs and hurriedly retraced his steps. Through the middle kitchen window he could just make out the open gate, the wooden ramp covering the steps and the first huge saddle-back sow ambling down into the yard. The pigs were being driven towards the back door.

Frankie dashed into the main kitchen and passed the window in a stoop to avoid being seen by the men outside. As he skirted the room to avoid the dogs, Rosie leaped against her chain and Lady hauled herself to her feet to join in the excitement. The outside door opened and a man entered the house just as Frankie slipped through the other door into the dark corridor beyond. He had taken only a few hasty steps when he heard the tread of feet on the wooden steps above his head. The Bogeyman. He shrank against the wall, felt himself embraced by coats hung one atop the other in untidy layers. Trapped between twin terrors, he allowed his body to sink within the folds of jackets and overcoats. One of his feet found its way into an enormous welling-ton boot. The other concealed itself in a discarded leather shoe. In seconds he was completely hidden, his heart pounding against his ribs and the fingers of his uninjured hand still grasping his precious newspaper.

In an almost soundless flurry of activity, the cellar door was opened and the light switched on to reveal the ramped steps. With little more than a few snorts and grunts, the lumbering animals were coaxed down the ramp. These were not the short-legged all-white animals that Buddie kept in his pigsties over by the disused cinder-heap. These pigs were taller and heavier, with a saddle of black colouring thrown across their backs and big metal clips attached to their ears. They did not squeal and race about in panic, but allowed themselves to be driven through the house and down the steep ramp to the underground slaughterhouse without protest.

Concealed amongst the coats, Frankie listened to the grunts of the animals and the low harsh voices of the men. The last pig was struggling to keep its footing on the ramp when the door to the best room opened and Smallfry stepped into the hall. She was wearing something pink and delicate that floated around her body when she moved. The fabric was so fine that she appeared to be naked in the bright light. At least four of the men were watching her as she stood in the hall, yawning prettily and obviously bewildered by the disturbance. Irish Tom detached himself from the group of workmen and swaggered, grinning, along the corridor.

'What is it?' Smallfry asked. 'What's happening?'

'Go back to bed, love. You'll be catching your death of cold out here in the hall wearing nothing but that little scrap of lace. Either that, or you'll be giving these dirty-minded men a lot of wicked ideas.'

'Oh, but I thought . . . . It was the noise . . . . It frightened me.'

Tom Fish looked back over his shoulder with a grin and a wink for his friends as his hand slid down the curve of her back to rest on the plump roundness of her buttocks. Gripping her in this coarse familiar fashion, he steered her into the room and closed the door with a gentle click behind him. The crude comments and laughter of the other men were cut short by a yelled command from the cellar. When Irish Tom re-emerged from the best room some minutes later, he was strutting like a peacock and rubbing the front of his pants in a suggestive manner.

Frankie felt his face redden and his hands clench themselves into fists. He could see Tom Fish standing like a huge black silhouette in the doorway, and he was tempted to rush forward and shove him head-first into the cellar below. Instead he tensed his whole body and tried to swallow the dryness in his throat. His belly was beginning to pull itself into painful spasms. He needed to go to the lavatory.

When at last he dared to creep from his hiding-place and move on tip-toe up the dark stairs, he had counted to 372 and managed to convince himself that any fate was preferable to having an accident down there amongst the coats. The upper rooms were silent when he finally went to his own room, but before getting into bed he pushed his wedge of broken chair-leg under the door to keep the Bogeyman out.

11

HE WAS NOT ALLOWED to go to school again until
Thursday morning, by which time the missing button
had been replaced on the collar of his shirt and he was
wearing a pair of smart new shoes of polished black
leather and knee-length grey socks with a dark red
band around their tops. Smallfry walked with him all
the way to the playground, where the other children
bunched together in little groups to stare at the absen-
tee and his beautiful mother. She looked different. Her
hair was done in pig-tails that hung over her shoulders
and were tied at the bottom with satin ribbon. She was
wearing a white dress with big navy-blue spots and a
tight white belt. Its skirt was so full that the slightest
movement caused it to swirl and lift about her legs.
Even her make-up was different. Today it made her
look pale and tired. She had dabbed powder over her
lipstick to rob it of its bright crimson lustre, and she
had forgotten the little pink patches of rouge that gave
her cheeks their rosy healthy glow. He had watched
her apply a smear of eye-black below her lower lashes,
then dust it with the palest face-powder until her eyes
appeared extra large and dark-rimmed. When Teacher
came out and rang his bell for the children to line up in
neat rows, she held Frankie back so that he was the
last to obey the signal. She smiled down at him in a
funny way, stroked his head, touched his cheek with
the back of her fingers. When she bent her head
towards his with her lips softly pouted, she came so

close that for one brief moment he thought she might actually kiss his forehead.

'Run along, my dear,' she murmured. 'Run along.'

Teacher was watching from the doorway when Frankie, the last child in his line, turned in time to see his mam move away from the school gate. Her hand fluttered in a small wave. She seemed to be limping very slightly, something he had failed to notice when they walked to school together.

To his complete amazement, Frankie found himself something of a minor celebrity among the children of St Andrew's. Three of the boys in his class were sporting recently shaved heads as pale and as smooth as newly laid eggs. One of the girls, the plump one with the freckles and the missing front tooth, looked very plain and dowdy now that she had lost all her pretty blonde curls. What remained of her hair had been clipped and plastered close to her head in a most unflattering style. She was sitting apart from those who had once been her friends, her eyes downcast and her cheeks blazing. Nobody wanted to share a desk with the only girl in the class with nits in her head.

Wally Watmough was the loud-mouthed fat boy who had once beaten Frankie almost senseless in a fist-fight behind the old air-raid shelter in a corner of the boys' playground. The quarrel had started over something as petty as who could spit furthest after eating half a ginger biscuit. Then Wally Watmough had called Frankie's mam a gypsy-woman and his dad a little black man, and the smaller boy, enraged, had attacked him without thought for the consequences. For his pains he received a black eye, a bloodied nose, a split lip, two skinned knees, several bruised ribs and four strokes of the cane on each hand for fighting on school premises. Now Wally Watmough made room at his desk for Frankie to sit beside him. Any boy who dared to venture down the Mucky Beck alone was deserving of great respect, even if he *had* fallen into the water and almost drowned.

A story was circulating around school that Frankie's mother had been very ill and one of his aunts was responsible for him having nits in his head and a dirty body, torn pumps, bitten nails and no dinner money. Smallfry had visited the school while Frankie was away. Everyone had seen her arrive during morning assembly, her hair hanging loose as she leaned on a heavy walking-stick for support. She had swooned in the main hall and had needed to be helped to the head-master's office and given water to drink and a damp cloth to cool her brow. Mr Sunderland himself had driven her home in his car, and she had begged him to leave her at the gate so as not to alarm her family. Everyone said she must have struggled from her sick-bed the moment she realized that the aunt left in charge during her illness had sadly neglected her little boy.

Alan Duffy had overheard Mr Simmons and Miss Craven talking about Frankie's father, who was a real-life American who had been in the Army and the merchant navy and was now a farmer who posed at the School of Art and played guitar in a popular local dance-band. They all knew about the big house in its own grounds and the genuine Yankee jeep his father drove. Someone even remembered seeing the famous photograph of Frankie on Trigger, his circus pony. Now everyone wanted to know him. His bruised hand was greatly admired and his escapade in Mucky Beck accepted as a terrific adventure. From being just another kid with nits in his head, the smallest in his class and the only one in the whole school whose skin was a swarthy brown, he suddenly found himself the most popular boy around.

101

'You must inform me if your mother becomes ill again. I had absolutely no idea things had become so difficult for her. She is a brave woman . . . a brave and very charming woman.'

'Yes, sir.'

Mr Sunderland scrutinized Frankie through narrowed eyes, his pursed expression implying that the brave and charming woman of his acquaintance deserved something better than the shabby little boy standing before him. He made tut-tutting sounds of disapproval through his teeth and fingered the fraying cuffs of his jacket. His dark pin-striped woollen suit was his uniform, the mute witness to countless terms dutifully served within the sombre walls of St Andrew's Junior School, Listerhills. The suit bore the wounds and scars of a lifetime's responsibilities in its faded knees and elbows, its sagging seat and greasy tired lapels.

'You must be good to your mother, Frankie,' he said now, using the stern long-suffering voice reserved for such interviews as this. 'And never forget that mothers are very precious people. We must always take special care of them.'

'Yes, sir.'

'And you must be grateful to her for everything she does, and for all the sacrifices she must make on your behalf. Remember that nothing in this world breaks a mother's heart like the raising of an ungrateful child.'

'Yes, sir.'

'And stay away from the beck. It's the stick for you, my lad, if you ever go down there again. Is that clear?'

'Yes, sir.'

'Right. Off you go, and don't let me hear any bad reports of you in the future.'

'Yes, sir . . . I mean . . . no, sir.'

Frankie left the headmaster's study feeling vaguely

troubled. Something was gnawing at the back of his mind. He felt that everything had changed during his brief absence from school. Even the teachers were being nice to him, and he did not understand why. It was late in the afternoon, during double English, that the answer came to him like a bolt out of the blue. Smallfry was sick. She was sick like the pretty lady in the film who went bravely on until she died all alone in her bed rather than compel her beloved family to share her pain. That must be the answer. His mam was dying of some rare disease which no doctor could cure and always, but always, proved fatal.

He ran all the way home after school. At Brooke Parker's there were men reversing a lorry against the bed of concrete that sloped down from the top of Thorpe Street to the wide loading-doors. He did not stop to watch the unloading. Instead he ran down the side of the building, past the high wall of its rear yard and through the gate leading to Old Ashfield. The Great Dane was tied up in the yard. Frankie peered around the angle of the wall, trying to measure the length of her chain before judging it safe to enter by the back door. She was lying in the mouth of the great arched chamber Buddie used as a tool-shed. Set between the shuttered window of the best room and the lower edge of the yard wall, the chamber sank back into the building like a huge stone tunnel. Inside on the left was a recessed door, now boarded and bolted, that once gave access to the best room. A similar door on the right was meant to serve the end house. The ground inside the arch was cobbled, and there were strangely shaped metal fittings set here and there into the walls. Buddie believed the original owner had kept his riding-carriage there, and the fittings were designed to house horse leathers and travelling gear, but Frankie was not so sure. He did not see why anyone, even a wealthy mill-owner, would want to drive a horse and carriage backwards down such a steeply sloping yard when he could just as easily leave it standing in the driveway.

Rosie had not noticed him. She was chewing savagely on something, making nasal snarling sounds as she ripped the thing apart with her sharp teeth. Frankie narrowed his eyes and squinted at the bloody object lying between her powerful front paws. It was brown and furry, like one of the big rats from the beck. He was still trying to identify it when he suddenly felt himself scooped from the ground and hoisted into the air in a wide arc.

'Whoopee . . . . Now, here's a fine young fellow if ever I saw one. In fact he's such a tall strapping chap that he calls his mam *Smallfry*. Isn't that so, Mr Big Man?'

Irish Tom's voice boomed with mirth and mockery below him as the airborne child flailed the air with his arms and legs. Rough hands gripped him by his crotch and the back of his neck, holding him aloft like a defenceless struggling insect tipped on to its back.

'*Smallfry*, indeed,' said another voice. 'And himself such a skinny little thing. Now, there's a *real* case of the stew-pan calling the kettle Grimy-arse.'

He could see very little, but the sound of their laughter told him a whole group of workmen had crept up on him while he was hugging the yard wall, fearful of the big Great Dane. Tom Fish held him at arm's length over his head, spun him this way and that until the sky turned sickeningly above him.

'Too high and mighty, he is, to call her "Mam", the way he should. Isn't that so, whelp?'

'Let me go. Put me down, you . . . you . . . . '

'Ha-ha, the whelp has fighting spirit. Tell us what you call your mam, boy. Come on, tell us all what you call your mam.'

Frankie felt himself gripped more tightly, then shaken so violently that his teeth rattled. Knowing that they would make fun of him, he had been very careful not to say her new name in front of Tom Fish. She must have told him herself. She could not possibly have known the misery such a revelation would cause him, because now he was forbidden to call her by any other name and he knew from painful experience that Tom Fish would not relent until he had his way.

'Smallfry,' he choked. 'Smallfry.'

'What? What was that? Speak up, big fellow, let's *all* be hearing it.'

'Smallfry . . . *Smallfry*.' He yelled the name as loudly as he could. In the roar of laughter it provoked, he felt himself falling swiftly towards the ground. He landed on his feet, hitting the narrow pavement outside the yard with such jarring impact that his teeth bit into the edge of his tongue. Tears stung his eyes. He felt small and feeble, hemmed in by five or six big broad-shouldered workmen. Irish Tom shoved him. He tripped and fell, scrambled to his feet and sprinted out of reach. The voice of the Irishman bellowed after him:

'Keep running, whelp. Let's see if you can make it all the way to the front door before Rosie gets you. I'm turning her loose right now. Keep running, kid. Here she comes. Go! Go! Go get 'im, Rosie! Go get 'im.'

The terrified Frankie skidded round the corner wall of the end house and raced as fast as his legs would carry him down towards the walkway gate. He could still hear the men yelling and laughing and whistling after him as he dragged the iron gate closed with a loud clang behind him. He made a dash for the big front door and threw himself into the gloomy chill of the hall. Panting, heart pounding, he stood back from the door and waited, safe in the knowledge that the dog was too big to squeeze herself through the gap allowed by the safety-chain. It was some time before he realized that he had been fooled. Rosie was not chasing him. The big Irishman had been teasing him all along, just to make him look ridiculous in front of all those other men. He had never intended to turn the dog loose, only to scare Frankie into scuttling for safety like a terrified rabbit running ahead of the hounds.

He seated himself on the cold tiles and picked at their dark dusty colours with one finger. There was a stinging spot on the side of his tongue where his teeth had sunk into the soft flesh. Last night he had dreamed yet again that the Irishman was doing dirty things in his mam's bed. It was the same dream as before, only this time Frankie had entered the room with his father's long-handled axe held high above his head. He had hacked at the man's naked backside until it fell away in bloody pieces ready to be thrown to the dogs. Smallfry's beautiful bed had become saturated with sticky red blood, but she had pulled Frankie into her arms and laughed and laughed with happiness because now the hated Tom Fish could never do dirty things to her again. Frankie had enjoyed the dream. It had left him with a feeling of self-satisfaction, a sense of having *done* something instead of standing helplessly in the shadows, aching with humiliation and guilty knowledge.

He got to his feet and walked on tip-toe to the kitchen door, where he pressed his face close to the crack, listening for any sound that might tell him what to expect. She was singing. He could hear her voice rising and falling to a tune called 'Sunny Side of the Street'. It was Buddie's signature tune, the one his band always played at the start of every session. It surprised Frankie that she rarely managed to sing all the words in the correct order. He would never

106

understand how she could memorize all those complex, impossibly long poems, yet forget the words of a simple song she must have heard a thousand times or more. She stopped singing when he knocked on the door, but he had to wait and knock a second time before she invited him in.

She was standing at the gas-stove, turning a plucked chicken over the flames to singe away the tiny feathers left behind in the skin. Other carcasses were trussed on the table, ready for cooking. He counted nine loaves of bread on the highest shelf and a dozen tins of meat stacked on the dresser. She smiled at him as she poured boiling water into his cup and stirred his cocoa into a miniature whirlpool with a spoon. She was wearing her rouge and bright red lipstick again, and the childish plaits were gone from her hair. Her eyes were bright and clear, no longer dark-rimmed.

'Omelettes for tea,' she smiled.

In a large bowl on the table was a thick mass of unlaid eggs taken from inside the chickens. Removed long before the shells had time to form, they were no more than a cluster of marble-sized orange balls in a thick yolky substance. When fried in the big iron pan they made an omelette that had a taste and a smell like nothing else in the whole world. Just thinking about it made his mouth water.

With a happy smile she resumed her work at the gas-cooker. He could see she was preparing for a party. The chickens would all be cooked by the next afternoon and allowed to cool on the pantry's cold slabs. Then the legs would be stacked on plates and the remainder of the meat sliced to make sandwiches. Frankie would be set to work at the big sink, and before he washed each plate and roasting-pan he would scrape it clean with his fingers and eat every last scrap of chicken, sage and onion stuffing, corned beef, sliced Spam and

107

cheese. Washing up was just one of the many benefits that usually came his way on party nights.

He watched her now as she singed the birds over the gas-flame. She did not look as if she might be dying of some dreadful disease. She looked perfectly healthy, but Frankie was not convinced. He would not be fooled like the man in the film who went cheerfully off to work, leaving his brave young wife to die all alone in their pretty country cottage.

12

BUDDIE WAS IN CHARGE at tea-time. He cut the bread into very thick slices and spread them so liberally with best butter that Frankie left a full set of toothprints behind with every bite. He cooked the omelettes until they were crisp and brown on the underside, firm and well set on top, exactly as Frankie liked them. To prevent any of the unlaid eggs from the party chickens going to waste, both father and son enjoyed an omelette inches thick and as wide in diameter as the big iron pan in which it was fried.

'You coming to my party tomorrow night, young fella?'

Frankie shifted his position on the high stool, frowned the way his father did and shrugged his shoulders in a very casual manner. The two of them were alone in the room, and Buddie was obviously speaking to him man-to-man. The least he could do in return was give the matter some serious consideration.

'I suppose so,' he said at last. 'If Smallfry says it's all right.'

'I'll square it with her. Are you sure you don't have anything better to do?' Buddie's face was solemn. A small pulse throbbed in his freckled brown cheek as it sometimes did when he was angry, or when he was trying his best not to laugh out loud at something. He chased the last piece of omelette around his plate with a fork. It slid over the edge and settled in a greasy stain on the table-cloth. He impaled it with a lunge, surveyed it thoughtfully, then popped it into his mouth and ground it between his teeth before washing it down with a swig of tea from his pint mug.

Frankie shrugged again and nodded his head, equally solemn. He, too, had a mug of tea. It was not so big as Buddie's, nor were the contents so strong and sweet, but he had been given tea rather than his usual cocoa, and that served to make him and his father two of a kind. He held the cup like Buddie, with the handle pointing at the middle of his forehead when he drank. After swallowing, he expelled his breath in a loud *aaaaah* and wiped the back of his hand across his mouth the way his father had just done.

'I think I *will* come,' he said at last. 'I'll probably wear my long trousers and my new bomber jacket . . . and my best leather shoes, of course.'

Buddie nodded gravely. The pulse in his cheek strengthened, and he cleared his throat with some force before asking: 'And will you be bringing along a chick, by any chance?'

'What?'

'A chick. A lady-friend. A *girl*.'

'Oh, a *chick* . . . . Well, I might ask Smallfry . . . . '

'Too late, young fella. She's already spoken for.'

Frankie reached for another slice of bread and butter, spooned sugar over it, tipped the surplus back into the sugar-bowl, then took a large bite and chewed it thoroughly before making his reply.

'In that case, I'll just come along in my own time and decide who to dance with when I get there.'

At this point, Buddie must have reached the thick layer of tea-leaves lining the bottom of his pint mug, because he suddenly began to cough and splutter as if something had slid down his throat the wrong way. Frankie reached over to thump his back, but Buddie clamped his hand over his mouth and dashed outside to the drain near the tool-shed. He closed the outer door behind him, and when Frankie saw him again he was laughing heartily, as if the prospect of almost choking on his tea-leaves had greatly amused him.

On Friday morning he went to school in the jeep, and as Buddie drove away with his horn blaring children surged across the playground in a boisterous rush to wave and yell until the little green vehicle was out of sight. Frankie stood in assembly feeling proud and special. It did not matter that he was standing in the back row, staring at a sea of backs and shoulders because he was so much shorter than all the other boys. He had a threepenny piece in his pocket and suddenly he was more popular than Wally Watmough, cock of the school, who lived above his father's bakery in Listerhills Road and brought tea-cakes and currant buns to school. He could even claim more friends than Donald Spinks, who became famous at Christmas when he fell through the ice on the old mill-pond and had to be rescued by three bobbies and the coal merchant's crew using all their empty coal-sacks and Mr Birkinshaw's ladder.

On his way home from school he took full advantage of his new-found prestige by showing off in front of the two boys who had walked with him along Shearbridge Road. First he climbed on to the wall of the steep ramp alongside the Bowling Green public house and, balancing with his arms outstretched like a tightrope-walker, inched his way up as far as the locked door behind which the barrels of beer were stored. Then he led his friends into the dark urinal set into the wall of the Corporation depot at the corner of Shearbridge and Great Horton Road. In the smelly interior they peed as noisily as possible before dashing outside and climbing the wall to stare at the great road-roller parked in the depot yard. They parted company at the row of tall

111

dingy red-brick houses behind which lay a labyrinth of cobbled streets. Frankie was glad he did not live in one of those tiny back-to-back houses like the other boys, with a cellar-head kitchen no bigger than a box and a lavatory outside in the yard.

Although the party was not due to begin until eight o'clock, things were already being organized in the enormous ground-floor room when Frankie arrived home that afternoon. From the front walkway he could look right in through what was the biggest window in the house with the nicest view of the trees and over-grown terraces. The hinged wooden shutters had been folded away into the panelled walls, the velvet drapes drawn back, the windows opened. In one corner of the room were grouped a few upright chairs and music-stands. The drums had been erected, the sheet music sorted into neat piles. Crates of beer and wine were stacked one atop the other in the big alcoves. Bottles of liquor stood together in neat ranks on the long marble shelf above the fireplace. Beside the big wind-up gramo-phone someone had placed two uneven towers of records in readiness for those intervals when the band rested. The front door had been thrown right back on its hinges, the tiled hall swept and mopped so that its colours glistened in the afternoon sunshine. Now the deeply embossed wallpaper, painted chocolate brown below its wooden dividing rail and a dull brownish cream above, could be seen in all its glory. It seemed to come to life in the sunlight, its sculpted surface depicting a multitude of flowers and ferns, leaves, insects and birds.

Upstairs on the landing, someone had positioned a heavy chest of drawers at the top of the small steps to prevent people wandering into the upper rooms. It stretched right across the landing from one side to the other, completely blocking off the Bogeyman's door and leaving only a small space near the banisters for Frankie to squeeze through. A light-bulb had been placed in the bathroom, with clean towels and perfumed soap and real crinkly lavatory-paper for the visitors to use. Outside in the yard, the dogs were tethered on shortened chains beneath the tool-shed's arch. The goats, too, had been safely penned for the occasion. In the main kitchen every surface was laden with plates and trays of sandwiches, chicken legs, biscuits and pastries.

Frankie had to kneel on a chair to reach the sink comfortably when he did the washing-up. He was left alone in the kitchen for a long time, so he was able to pick the chicken carcasses clean before he threw them in the bin. With a tablespoon he ate all the jelly Small-fry had scraped from the tinned meat. By the time the dishes were washed and dried and returned to their shelves, he needed only a single slice of bread-and-sugar and two pieces of broken biscuit to complete his evening meal. As a safeguard against late-night hunger, he buttered two thick end-pieces from a loaf, wrapped them in greaseproof paper and carried them up to his room concealed inside his shirt. He was careful not to touch the food already arranged on the plates. Every item would be accounted for. She would know at a glance if anything went missing. He would not fall into that particular trap a second time.

The music was playing when he came downstairs wearing his new leather shoes and his bomber jacket. People were already crowding into the big room and talking together in the hall. Some were sitting outside, where cushions and folded blankets had been placed on the wide rounded steps serving the front door. One of his aunts was laughing while Buddie played his guitar and sang the words of a song as if they were meant specially for her. Frankie wondered if this was the aunt who had

113

neglected him, the one who should have come to the house to take care of him when Smallfry discovered that she was very ill. He liked this aunt. She was small and brown like Buddie, so everyone could see that they were brother and sister. She smiled a lot and cuddled Frankie against her soft breasts and did not seem to mind that he was so short and thin for his age. He hoped she was not the one who had let Smallfry down so badly and caused him to get nits in his head.

He was glad when Blossom arrived because she was so happy and noisy and funny that she made everyone laugh. She was wearing a figure-hugging red dress and little silk roses pinned to her hair in such a way that they appeared to be sprouting like real flowers from the frizzy black mass in which her face was framed. She had painted her lips with cyclamen-pink lipstick that made her huge mouth seem even larger. Each time she laughed she threw back her head with a piping shriek to show the biggest, whitest teeth and the very pinkest gums imaginable. She had brought a friend to the party, a man several inches shorter than herself who spoke with a strange accent and had a very odd way of dancing because he came from the West Indies where they drank a lot of rum. His skin was almost the same colour as his dark brown jacket. Were it not for the crisp white collar of his shirt, it would have been difficult to see where the jacket ended and his skin began.

There were only five men playing in the band, including Buddie who also sang the songs. Early in the evening one of the men became too drunk to play his saxophone and had to be helped into the kitchen, where he collapsed in a chair and later vomited all over his shoes and socks. Another man started to dance with one of the pretty young women from the Art School, and then he did not want to play in the band any more because she kept asking him to stay with her instead.

114

'Here's a half-crown from Nanny and another one from me. That's five whole shillings, just for yourself, and not a word to anyone.'

Frankie squirmed and giggled as his aunt's hot breath and soft lips tickled the inside of his ear. She had pushed two coins into the pocket of his bomber jacket. His eyes widened as his fingers closed around them. He could identify them even without looking, just by their size and thickness, and by the ladder-like lines etched into their outer edge. They were definitely half-crowns. He suddenly felt like a rich man. His aunt had danced away, wiggling and swinging her plump backside in time to the music, before he could thank her for the gift.

Big Tom Fish looked very different with his hair slicked down and his grubby working-clothes exchanged for a dark suit and a smart white tie. He wore shoes instead of boots, and his hands had been scrubbed until they resembled the hands of a man who worked with clean things. Frankie noticed how the women followed him with their eyes and smiled up into his face in that way women do when they want men to notice them. Irish Tom was a very handsome man, and Frankie hated him the more because everyone else seemed to be taken in by his smile and his twinkling eyes, his gentle manner and soft lilting accent.

Tom had a younger brother called Jack, whose ginger hair was thick and untidy and whose face had become creased and chubby from continuous smiling. His eyes were hooded, giving him a sleepy carefree expression. His knuckles were always skinned because he drank a lot of beer and whisky and then wanted to fight with everyone he saw, be they friend or enemy. It was Jack who secretly gave Frankie the bottle of strong beer and the glass of home-made lemonade laced with vodka.

When the party was in full swing, the rooms throbbed with music and the whole house seemed to be filled

115

with the babble of loud happy voices. Cigarette-smoke drifted about in blue clouds, and everywhere the crush and the smell of dancing bodies added to the excitement of the evening. Buddie encouraged the boy to go through his whole repertoire of dance-steps from waltz to boogie while several guests stood around in a tight little circle, clapping and cheering him on. By the time his head began to swim and his eyes to sting in the smoky atmosphere, his pockets were weighted down and jingling with coins. He was extremely happy because Buddie had called him 'Mr Bo Jangles' and laughed and roared and winked because his son was the best goddam dancer at the party.

Frankie wandered out to the front steps and sat there for a long time, breathing in the cool night air and hoping he would not be sick all over like the saxophone-player in the kitchen. He sipped his beer straight from the bottle. It was bitter and gassy, but it was a real grown-up drink and he could not possibly admit, even to himself, that he found the taste disagreeable. When he closed his eyes his whole body seemed to be spinning round in circles, a sensation so convincing that he was constantly surprised to discover himself still sitting quite firmly on the edge of the step.

When Smallfry made her grand entrance the band had just started to play her favourite song, 'Golden Ear-Rings'. She swept from the best room wearing a dress of green velvet that Frankie had never seen before. Her shoes were very high, with straps around the ankles and something bronze, with tiny pin-points of bright green, flashing from each cut-away front. Her waist was pinched inside a broad black belt, her bare neck and shoulders creamy pale against the rich colour of her gown. Frankie had never seen her look more beautiful. Every head turned as she glided through the

116

crowded company, smiling and fluttering her lovely eyes at all the male guests. As if to illustrate the words of her favourite song, glistening gold ear-rings on wire hooks dangled from her ears to brush lightly against her shoulders each time she moved her head. In the light her glorious hair shone like burnished copper, and Frankie knew that the look of pride on his father's face was mirrored in his own. His Smallfry, his Sweetheart, his Mam, was without doubt the loveliest lady in the whole wide world.

Frankie's legs were wobbly when he tried to stand. He stumbled as far as the main staircase before flopping down on one of the cold stone steps to take another sip from his bottle of beer. From there he could see Smallfry laughing and swaying to the music in the big room, and he was glad that Tom Fish had missed her special entry. He had already seen the grinning Irishman going down into the garden with someone who looked like one of the girls from the big school, rather than a proper grown-up. The steps were mossy and cracked in places where grass and weeds had grown right through the stone. With any luck the Irishman would miss his footing in the dark and break his neck in a fall.

Chuckling to himself, Frankie swallowed another mouthful of beer and released the gas from his body in a hefty burp. Then he hauled himself to his feet and struggled to make his legs carry him upstairs to the lavatory, where he could be as sick as he liked without shaming his parents or making a terrible spectacle of himself.

13

HE REMEMBERED being sick. It left a pain in his chest
and an emptiness in his belly that made him think of
eating, yet the more he thought about it the less the
prospect appealed to him. He could also recollect tearing lavatory-paper from the roll one sheet at a time
and smoothing it across his knee until he had collected
a sizeable pile. This he took to his room and hid
between the pages of a comic on the window-ledge
behind the blackout curtain. Too tired to count all the
money from his pockets, he had wrapped it in newspaper and hidden it in a tiny gap behind the wardrobe.
The next thing he remembered was waking up to find
his head throbbing and his mattress wet in two places.
He knew he had been asleep for a long time because
the sky was beginning to lighten and the house no
longer resounded with party sounds.

Downstairs the guests who remained had split themselves into sleepy drinking groups or fallen asleep in
chairs and corners. The kitchen door was open. People
were sitting around the big table with wine-glasses
and playing cards, or slumped in chairs with their eyes
closed and their mouths gaping open. Two men were
arguing about petrol coupons; another about gypsies
stealing all the scrap iron from his garden shed. He
could see Smallfry sitting stiffly in her high-backed
chair. She looked pale and tired and very, very angry.
Something scraped beneath his shoe on the bottom
step, slid over the edge and landed with a metallic

clatter on the tiles. He stooped to retrieve it, turned it over and over in his fingers so that the green spots twinkled in the light from the hall. It was a bronze frog, about two and a half inches in length, with a roughened body, bent legs and perfectly shaped toes with knuckles like human fingers. Its eyes were two shiny green stones that flashed with reflected light. It was one of the decorations from Smallfry's shiny black patent-leather shoes. He could see the little bar on its under-side and a scrap of cotton from the stitching that had held it in place. She was probably angry and upset because she had lost it. He smiled. He would soon put the radiant smile back on her face.

He walked to the kitchen a little unsteadily, conscious of the great mounds of coats clinging like a colony of bats to the wall on his left. He stepped over outstretched feet and handed the bronze frog to Smallfry. She snatched it from his hand, then glared down at him with her lips tightened into a narrow unattractive line.

'I found it in the hall,' he offered softly, not really sure why he was whispering. 'It isn't broken, Smallfry. It just fell off your shoe because the stitching came loose.'

'What the hell are you doing down here at four o'clock in the morning?' She hissed the question through clenched teeth. 'I won't have you creeping about the house, listening at doors and spying on me. Get out of my sight. Go on, get upstairs to bed, you little sneak.'

Bitterly disappointed, Frankie turned and left the kitchen in silence. He knew better than try to protest his innocence. She always called him a liar when he tried to explain things, and her anger made him so nervous that he stammered and stuttered until his shortcomings sent her into a screaming rage. He would

119

rather suffer the short sharp sting of rejection than risk the full weight of her temper.

Someone had switched out the light on the half-landing outside the bathroom door. Frankie sat there in the darkness, listening to the sounds from downstairs. A number of cheering people suddenly burst from the party room and staggered outside. Like a small brown prancing Pied Piper, Buddie led them away from the house in a merry dance. Their voices echoed along the terrace to become muffled by distance once the happy group had passed through the wrought-iron gate and out into the more open area beyond. Frankie was afraid to follow them because Smallfry had ordered him to go to bed. She would only punish him in secret tomorrow or the next day, or even next week, if he went against her wishes. He recalled the only time he had dared ask Buddie to take him out in the jeep. She had forbidden the trip almost before the words had passed his lips, but Buddie had laughed his big laugh and told him to jump aboard and even allowed him to wear his funny peaked cap with the winged badge on the side. Smallfry had waved them off happily enough, and Frankie had enjoyed one of the most exciting days of his life. They had visited a farm with real sheep, and another where he was allowed to ride a pony to prove to the man how well Buddie had taught him to handle a horse. Then they had driven a long way across the moors to see a man called Roger, who had twin sons called James and Andrew, a dog that did not bite or snarl and a barn filled to its great rafters with prickly sweet-smelling hay. All afternoon they had played in the barn while the men talked business. They had climbed the outside ladder to the top window and leaped through into the hay with enough force to send them skidding right to the far side of the barn, down the long wooden shoot to ground-level, across the floor and out the front door in one noisy, exhilarating, unforgettable ride. Roger was not even a little bit cross when he saw how much straw was littering the ground outside the barn door. They had eaten scones for tea and beef dripping spread on home-made bread. It had been a wonderful day, a day in which Frankie had not disgraced himself either by twitching his face or by stammering when he spoke. Smallfry had seemed pleased that he had had such a good time with Buddie, but later that night she had called him downstairs and thrashed his bottom with the back of a hair-brush until he danced about the room in pain and was unable to sit down for hours. She promised to take a stick to him if he dared go against her wishes ever again, and to put him in a *Home* if he told his father about the thrashing.

Frankie's head jerked, startling him awake. He had fallen asleep on the darkened half-landing with his back against the wall, legs drawn up and hugged by both arms, cheek resting on his knees. He heard shrieks of laughter and snatches of song as Buddie and his friends passed once more along the front terrace. He guessed that they were dancing round and round the outside of the house in the moonlight, playing adult games impossible for him to understand.

Suddenly another sound, closer and more ominous, caused him to stiffen with anxiety. On the opposite side of the landing, movement stirred within the mildewed old mirror. He rubbed sleep from his eyes and stared at the vague reflected images trapped in the glass. A crack had appeared at the outer edge of the Bogeyman's door. As it slowly widened, a shaft of flickering light spread across the wall. Frankie looked to his right. From his corner he could see nothing but the hulking shape of the chest of drawers blocking the landing and the eerie light lengthening along the wall.

121

He looked back at the mirror, which was set at an angle in the far corner of the half-landing and told a very different story. In it he could see a thick candle appearing through the widening gap in the Bogeyman's door, held aloft by a sinewy white hand which in turn was attached to a stringy wrist. It looked like the hand of a skeleton; all knuckle and bone with absurdly long fingers. Frankie held his breath and stared with growing horror at the dark glass. The shadow of the Bogeyman slowly materialized: a long gaunt profile with a pointed nose and narrow domed head. It was followed by a face as waxy-white as the shadow was black. The features were scrawny, flesh-less, a death-mask with shadowed eye-sockets. The apparition quivered in the candle's unsteady light. It was horrible. It must be a zombie, or a bloodless vampire hungry for warm living flesh. Somehow Frankie knew that if it managed to move beyond the confines of the old mirror it would be free to roam the house at will. With a loud yell he pushed himself away from the wall and went clattering down the steps and out the front door as if the Devil himself was on his heels. Upstairs a door slammed, a key turned hastily in a lock and several stout bolts were slid back into place on the inside of the Bogeyman's door.

It was cold outside. The air was damp and heavy with the scents of growing things; not flowery and sweet but pungent and earthy and green. Moonlight glittered in silver flashes between the branches of the trees and lay in a soft sheen on the crazy paving. He could hear Buddie and his friends beyond the terrace gate. They were gathered at the top of the hill where the ground fell away in a steep hazardous drop to the Mucky Beck. Frankie arrived there in time to see his father make a flying leap for the Tarzan swing. His hands grabbed at the stout rope, his feet closed around the bulky knot. In one smooth movement his agile body hurtled into the gap between the trees, turned in mid-air and swept back to drop nimbly on to safe ground at the top of the hill. A few cheers and a ripple of applause accompanied his stunt. Frankie grinned from his quiet spot just a few feet away. Buddie had made a good swing, as good as any Frankie had managed to achieve.

The next person to try the swing was the cheerful black man who had come to the house with Blossom. Instead of reaching up to grab the rope as far from the bottom as possible, he took hold of the knot in both hands and, before anyone could stop him, lurched into space like a blind man with a death-wish. He crashed into the nearest tree, bounced off to one side, entangled his legs in the branches of a second tree and plummeted to the ground with a crash. Invisible in the darkness, he bounced all the way to the bottom of the hill without so much as a whisper of protest, and there he lay, silent and motionless.

In the deadly hush that followed the fall, the amiable Irish Jack, brother of Tom Fish, set down his bottle of whiskey and lumbered forward to try his own skills on the swing. He clasped his hands high up the rope, as Buddie had done, and swung himself into the same pitch-black gap between the trees. Then his grip weakened and his big hands slid down the rope, bounced over the knots and came back together in a clap, gripping nothing but empty air. With a loud and profane curse, he hit the hillside and rolled, carrying twigs and rubble and piles of loose earth, to the wall at the bottom of the hill.

All of a sudden there was pandemonium on the hillside. Men began to shout and women to scream as moans of pain drifted up from the darkness. Someone ran back to the house for a flashlight, while two men

123

who knew the outbuildings hurried to the pigsties for a coil of rope and a long ladder. Then Buddie scrambled down the hill in search of the fallen men. He found them lying quite close together, their falls broken by a tangle of tree-roots and a rusting car-body. Blossom's boyfriend was bleeding and only semi-conscious. His left leg had been twisted under his body at a peculiar angle, and the blood glistening on the side of his head looked like thick black oil in the torch-light. Irish Jack had burned all the skin from his hands, leaving his palms and fingers raw and bloody. Both men had to be hauled back to level ground with the help of the jeep's winch, a sheet of tarpaulin, several lengths of rope and a great many shouted instructions. A full hour was to pass before the jeep drove off to the Royal Infirmary and those who were left behind wandered back to the house, the exciting interlude at an end.

Frankie followed the group at a safe distance and positioned himself on a chilly step halfway up the main staircase. Although all movement had now ceased behind the Bogeyman's door, nothing would induce the boy to make the long dark journey along the upper corridor to his room. Instead he gripped the banisters and stared through the open kitchen door, and after a few moments his attention became riveted on the scene before him.

The pretty young woman who had gone down into the garden with Tom Fish was now crying noisily. Her hair was all messed up, her blouse soiled and torn along one of its shoulder-seams. There were green stains on the back of her skirt that might have been caused by damp grass, and one of her nylon stockings was badly laddered.

'You shouldn't have done that,' Irish Tom was shouting. 'It's a terrible thing, the two of you fighting and scratching and screaming like alley cats, and you a married woman and all.'

He was shouting at Smallfry. Through the lower banisters Frankie could see her standing in the kitchen, wringing her hands together the way she did whenever she was particularly upset. Her long hair, so beautifully styled only a few hours ago, now hung loose and untidy around her face. One of her lovely gold ear-rings was missing.

'Get that little tramp out of my house,' she said in a shrill voice.

'Now, come on, woman. Where's the sense in all this silly jealousy?'

'I want that whore out of my house, and she can count herself damn lucky I don't turn the dogs on her.'

'All right. All right. I'll take her home.'

'You most certainly will *not*,' Smallfry exclaimed, rounding on Tom Fish with her fists clenched and her eyes flashing.

'Oh, for the love of Mike . . . . '

'You'd like that, wouldn't you? You'd just *love* to get your little tart all alone in the back of your van, you dirty Irish bastard.'

'Will you at least keep your voice down so the whole damn house doesn't have to suffer the wickedness of that tongue of yours?'

In the scuffle that followed, Frankie was not quite certain what happened. He saw Smallfry reach for the young woman's face with both hands, her fingers bent like talons. Tom Fish stepped between them and received a resounding slap to his face. He instantly returned the slap with enough force to throw Smallfry backwards across the kitchen table. She screamed, leaped to her feet and launched herself at the big man with her fingernails clawing at his face. Amid the screeches and bellows of rage, the unfortunate young woman, sobbing loudly, rushed from the room, slamming the door behind her. Frankie was left to crouch on the stairs with their angry voices ringing in his ears and the sounds of a heated and very violent battle coming from the kitchen. He covered his ears with both hands. He was frightened. He wanted to help Smallfry but did not know what to do, or even if she would appreciate his interference.

When he could bear it no longer he crept into the music-room, where the gentle rhythm of a man's snores and the steady ticking of a clock were more comforting to his ears. He pulled two cushions and a large blanket into the space between the music-stands and chairs, curled himself into a tight ball and closed his eyes. He wondered what had happened to the Bogeyman, the fleshless zombie-like creature in the upstairs room, and to the two men who had fallen from the Tarzan swing, and to the unhappy young woman out there alone in the grounds of Old Ashfield. He tried not to think about the screams and slaps and crashes he could still hear coming from the kitchen. His mind was spinning and his heart thudding with apprehension, but he was unaware of the outcome of the fracas or the length of time for which it raged. Some time in the early dawn, with his index fingers pressed deep into his ears and his eyes screwed tightly closed, he fell asleep in the safest corner of the music-room.

14

IT WAS FULL DAYLIGHT when the men came in to clear the
room. Sunshine slanted through the big window, tossing brilliant reflections over everything and creating
beams that danced and shimmered with trapped dust.
Frankie saw for the first time that the linoleum was
shabby and badly worn in places, and that the floor-
boards in the alcoves were as stained and damaged as
those in his own room. He hid behind the gramophone
cabinet, still wrapped in his warm blanket, while two
men gathered up the music-stands and piled the song-
sheets into a cardboard box. Everything had to be
packed away in the big truck because the full band had
been booked to play two nights at a dance-hall in
Brighouse. They dragged out the crates stacked with
empty beer- and wine-bottles and left them outside the
front door for the pub men to collect later in the day.
Then they unfastened the panels on each side of the
window and pulled out the shutters. Once the hinges
were fully extended and the locks in place, only the
merest sliver of sunlight was allowed to filter into the
room through tiny spaces in the wood. With the door to
the hall closed, the blackout was complete. Frankie
was oddly saddened by the ease with which light and
warmth and the nicest season of the year could be
banished from a room in favour of a chilly, unfriendly
darkness.

When the men had gone he tip-toed upstairs. Having
served its purpose, the bulky chest of drawers had been

dragged from the landing into one of the first-floor rooms. The Bogeyman's door was closed, the upper corridor in darkness. Everything was back to normal.

In the bathroom he turned on the cold tap and hung head-first over the edge of the basin to drink. He was unbearably thirsty. His head ached, and his mouth was coated with such a thick unpleasant taste that he was surprised to find no visible signs of disease when he stared at himself, mouth stretched open to its limit and tongue protruding as far as it would go, in the broken piece of mirror in the lavatory. Someone had peed in the corner beside the pot, leaving a large pool stagnating on the linoleum. The stink reminded him of the gents' urinal in Shearbridge Road where he and his friends had gone in defiance of the headmaster's warnings. Mr Sunderland believed that all the men's urinals in Bradford were places of great danger since two schoolboys were attacked in Little Horton and another in West Bowling only a year ago.

He found a cake of toothpaste in a flat round tin in the bathroom, selected a toothbrush from the window-ledge, dampened it with water and rubbed the cake into a pink froth. It had a sharp minty taste, and the more he brushed, the more nastiness he managed to clean from his mouth. He washed his hands and face in cold water. The new soap had been left in a wet saucer so that a layer of slime had formed on its under-side. It smelt of roses and something even sweeter, like violets. He wiped the soap and tipped the slime from the saucer because it was a shame to waste nice things.

He returned downstairs and went through his usual practice of listening at every keyhole. He expected the house would be quiet all day following the late and very rowdy party. Adults liked to sleep late on Saturdays. If the dogs were still tied and the goats penned, he would go out to play in the gardens. He could spend some

128

time on the Tarzan swing and then collect a few tin cans from the bottom of the hill to use as target practice. For his last birthday, Buddie had made him a bow and a quiver of metal-tipped arrows with real feathered flights. He was a good shot. Sometimes he drew a face on a sheet of paper, pinned it to the trunk of a tree and pretended it was Irish Tom eating his sandwiches in the garden. Doing that made him a much better shot. He could always hit the target ten times out of ten by pretending he was repaying Tom Fish for past hurts and humiliations.

As he tip-toed through the house there were two things uppermost in his mind. He needed to know that Smallfry was all right after her terrible quarrel with the Irishman, and he wanted to see what food remained after the party. He had two slices of bread hidden away in his room, but that would not be enough if Buddie was to be away and Smallfry was still in a bad mood from last night. She might not call him down from his room the whole day, and then it would be too late to expect more than cocoa for his supper. Any left-over sandwiches and chicken would be given to the dogs unless Frankie could get to them first.

He stood outside Smallfry's door for a long time, his ear pressed to the keyhole and his eyes closed in concentration. He heard nothing. At least he could be sure that Tom Fish, with his grunts and snores and obscene animal noises, was not inside the room.

He took particular care before entering the kitchen. He got down on his hands and knees and peered beneath the door. He could see the linoleum covering most of the stone flags, and the sacking where the dogs normally slept. The lower inches of the table-legs were hung with curls of stringy black cotton where strands from the mop attached themselves to the wood each time the floor was cleaned. He could see all this

129

because the door-curtain was not in place and the sausage-shaped mat had not been pressed to the bottom of the door on the inside. What he saw convinced him that Smallfry was not in the room. She hated draughts. Draughts and cold places made her ill. She would never sit in the kitchen with the curtain pulled back and the gap uncovered at the bottom of the door.

He had been right about the food. There were plenty of leftovers for him to pick at. He pulled meat and cheese out of sandwiches grown crisp from standing all night in the hot room. One of the small pastries he took contained sweet mincemeat that stuck to his newly brushed teeth. Another was packed with slices of juicy cooked apple and topped with a layer of crunchy sugar. He drank milk straight from the big jug on the pantry shelf, and all the time his attention was constantly drawn to a bottle of lemonade lying on its side on the seat of a chair. He believed he could hide it in his room and nobody would ever suspect that he had taken it. And it would not *really* be stealing, because all the food and drink had been laid out so that everyone could help themselves to anything they wanted. Frankie had been specially invited to the party by Buddie himself; and, although Smallfry always insisted that he was entitled to *nothing*, as one of the guests he should be allowed to help himself without fear of being branded a thief. He was almost one hundred per cent sure that his logic was sound. Even so, he decided to err on the side of caution and sneak the bottle of lemonade to his room without being seen.

The dogs were still tied up in the arched mouth of the tool-shed. He had never known them to be so quiet and well behaved for such a long time. Buddie swore that no dog in the world barked or growled for as many hours a day as Rosie. He must have given her a lot of meat and biscuits to keep her so quiet for the last two days. Lady was asleep on her side with her legs sprawled out and her big barrel chest heaving as she breathed. The Great Dane was leaping about with something in her mouth that she threw into the air from time to time, grabbed in her teeth and shook violently, then pounded into the ground with her front paws. Frankie rubbed at the window with his fingers to make a clean patch, then leaned across the sink to peer into the yard. After a while he rubbed a bigger patch and stared again. At first he thought she must be catching rats and killing them in the same cruel way cats like to kill mice. Then he realized that the legs he could see here and there in the yard were too big and furry to have been torn from dead rats. A discarded body thrown against the wall, ripped but still identifiable, confirmed his suspicions. Rosie had killed her babies. The cardboard box was lying on its side, empty. What remained of her litter of five pedigree Great Dane pups was strewn about the yard in a scattering of bloody scraps.

Frankie gathered up his store of food, heaved the bottle of lemonade into his arms and hurried back upstairs. He did not want to be around when someone discovered what Rosie had done.

He played on the Tarzan swing until his hands were filthy and his arms tired and he had proved to his own satisfaction that nobody, not even Buddie, could handle the swing with quite the same measure of expertise as himself. Then he slithered down to the spot at the bottom of the hill where the two men had fallen during the night. Rummaging around in the dirt and debris, he was lucky enough to find a shilling and two sixpences, a drawing of Queen Victoria and a Craven 'A' packet with four cigarettes still inside. A little further down he found a man's wristwatch with a broken strap and a badly scratched face. When he held it to his ear the steady ticking told him that it was still in working order in spite of the fall and several hours spent lying on the damp earth. Frankie was delighted. He had always wanted a watch or a clock of his very own so he would not be late for school when Smallfry called him at the wrong time. He hated to be late for school, especially on those mornings when he missed assembly altogether because he had to take milk-bottles back to the shop to raise money for his dinner and neither Bland's nor Midgley's opened before the very last stroke of nine o'clock. He had a feeling that the watch was going to change his life. He did not even mind that the strap was broken and refused to fasten around his wrist. He would keep it in the pocket of his new bomber jacket.

It was precisely three twenty-six in the afternoon when she called him. Her voice sounded weak and distant, as if it came from a long way away. He wondered if she was ill because she had found the half-eaten puppies in the yard, or if the party had left her feeling sick and dizzy, the way parties often did because she was very sensitive to rough-and-ready people and noisy atmospheres. As he descended the big stairs he saw that the door of the best room had been opened. A blazing fire burned in the grate, adding its light to that of the twin lamps positioned close to the alcove where her bed was set.

'Frankie . . . come to me, Frankie . . . '

The breath caught in the boy's throat. He could tell by the sound of her voice that she was very ill.

'Frankie . . . my son . . . come closer . . . let me see you . . . ' Her voice faded into silence, and she coughed delicately. Her pale hand raised itself from the bed, only to flop back like a limp flower, devoid of all strength.

Frankie entered the hot stuffy room and was shocked

132

to the core by what he saw. He was looking at the death scene from *Woman of Courage*, which had starred a very pretty actress who looked a lot like Smallfry but not nearly so beautiful. The bed had been draped with white sheets that hung in fluted folds all the way from the picture-rail above the brass bed-ends to the floor, where another white sheet completely concealed the patterned rug. A pile of soft white pillows with barely a crease in their cases supported her head and shoulders. She was wearing a flowing white nightdress with frothy lace at the bodice and cuffs, and her lower body was covered by the soft white coverlet with the snow-flake lace and pretty silk fringe. This was her deathbed. It was exactly like the one in the film where the poor actress had died after making her last, sad speech.

'I can't go on any longer. I'm dying,' she whispered.

'No, Smallfry . . . no . . . '

'Be brave, my son . . .' She coughed again. She lay in a haze of Californian Poppy, her face ashen, lips colourless, eyes dark-rimmed. Her hair looked as if it had been carefully brushed into a huge copper fan across the white pillows. She looked like an angel, a poor dying angel. 'Oh, my sweet, sweet child . . . what will become of you when I'm gone?'

'M-Mam . . . ,' he stammered. 'S-Smallfry . . . '

Frankie's whole body began to tremble. He stared at the vision of pale fragility on the shrouded bed. She was dying. His mam was dying, and he did not know what to do, how to help her. He wanted to fling himself across her bed and tell her that he loved her and she was the most precious and beautiful person in the whole world, but he knew she did not like to be touched. Instead he just stood there with tears streaming from his eyes and his face twitching in nervous spasms.

'Don't d-die,' he stammered. 'Please don't d-die.'

133

'Oh, how it pains me to leave you . . . . '

'D-Don't, Mam . . . don't leave me . . . Smallfry . . . don't die.'

'You never loved me . . . any of you . . . . '

'I did, we do . . . honest . . . honest . . . I do.'

'I was never really appreciated . . . . '

'Oh, you were . . . you w-were,' he protested, and suddenly he was sobbing, terrified that she was about to die and leave him to be put in a *Home* with all the other motherless children that nobody wanted.

'You'll be sorry when I'm gone . . . all of you . . . sorry when I'm . . . when I'm . . . dead.' She tried to raise herself but fell back against the pillows with a sigh. 'Now go . . . go and leave me in peace. I want to be alone.'

'Don't . . . oh, please . . . p-please don't . . . . '

'Leave me . . . . '

Frankie backed towards the door. He saw her raise herself for the last time, touch her hand to her brow and sigh as if even that small effort sapped her fading strength.

'Tell nobody,' she whispered. 'Nobody . . . do you understand?'

'Oh, Smallfry . . . . '

'Not a soul. You must speak of this to *nobody*. If you love me at all . . . *really* love me . . . you'll grant me this one final wish . . . that I be permitted to die in peace.'

By now his sobs were loud and ragged, shaking his body so that he could barely breathe. He was distraught. He watched her frail hand pluck weakly, distractedly at the snowy bed-cover.

'M-Mam . . . M-Mam . . . . '

'Go . . . leave me . . . I want to be alone . . . . '

He stepped into the open doorway.

'You never loved me . . . You'll all be sorry when I'm gone . . . Oh . . . Oh . . . '

With a strangled cry Frankie turned and rushed from the room. As he ran upstairs his own voice rang in his ears, loud and anguished. He did not care that his choking sobs might be heard by the Bogeyman or the stranger who lived in the attic. She was dying. He had seen how it happened on the big screen at the Empire, and now the same terrible thing was happening to her. Her hand would be cold and limp and her body very still when everyone filed into the room to weep over her later, when she had breathed her last and gone to heaven and would not have to suffer in this life any more.

Blinded by tears, he threw himself into his room and collapsed across his own bed, his body racked with sobs. His life was over, finished. He was going to be an orphan. Smallfry was dying.

15

RAIN was pattering on the glass like urgent fingers. A fretful wind, uncertain of its bearings, lashed the branches of the big tree in every direction and back again as if working itself into a frenzy. His watch had stopped at ten minutes to eight, but whether that was morning or evening he had no way of knowing. As he drifted up from sleep the sudden awareness of what had recently taken place filled his insides with an agony of distress. By now his mam was certainly lying cold and dead in the room downstairs. He was already an orphan. It was just a matter of time before the men from the *Home* came to take him away.

The pain inside welled up into his throat and spilled from him in a sound that was part wail, part groan. There was a nasty taste in his mouth because he had made himself sick with crying, and now he could smell his vomit on the edge of the mattress and on the floor beside the bed. He felt that he, too, was dying, that the sense of hollowness within him was growing and spreading and eating him away until soon his body would collapse in on itself like an empty useless shell.

He had once come home from school to find her sitting in a chair with several boxes of pills tipped into her lap and a strange, almost wild expression on her face. She had told him her life was in ruins and she would be better off dead, and he had pleaded and wept and begged her not to kill herself by taking any more of the pills. On a number of occasions she had dressed herself in her very best frock and jewellery and positioned herself on the floor with her head resting on a pillow inside the gas-oven. She had insisted that he watch her die because he was the cause of all her troubles, and once he had fainted and cut his head on the stone floor when the limpness of her body and the glassy stare in her eyes convinced him that she was really dead. Now the decision was no longer hers to make. Now the mysterious disease had overtaken her, and it was all Frankie's fault. He knew without doubt that she had died because of him. She had often explained to him how very sensitive people fade away when they are unhappy, especially beautiful talented ladies who are dragged down in life by cruel circumstances and an ungrateful child.

With his face twitching and his front teeth tearing at already bitten-down fingernails, Frankie paced to and fro across the darkened room, his mind casting about for something different to dwell on, something that might distance him, however temporarily, from his present predicament. He forced himself to think of Maureen, the dark-haired lady in the ticket office of the Empire picture-house. She wore costumes with fitted jackets to emphasize her small waist, and blouses with layers of lace at the neck to hide an unsightly purple birthmark. Smallfry had pierced her ears with a darning needle and a cork to prevent the point from sticking into her neck when it reached the other side. Within a few days, both lobes had swelled and turned horribly septic, and Maureen had been forced to stay in bed for almost two whole weeks because her blood had become poisoned. Now that her ears were healed and her blood cured, she chose to wear ear-rings with clips at the back or little screws that could be adjusted for a comfortable fit. The holes in Smallfry's ears had been there for so long that they were stretched to slits because the big ear-rings she loved to wear were very heavy. She feared that one day her lobes would tear right down to the bottom and she would need to have them pierced again in a different place. She did not mind the pain and the risk of blood poisoning because she enjoyed being stylish and different, and not a soul in Bradford had ever seen jewellery quite like hers.

Frankie urged his mind to grasp at any thought, any memory strong enough to convince him that his mam was still alive. It seemed to him that she was the foundation on which his whole existence depended. She dominated his life. She provided the roof over his head and the food in his belly and the love and care that kept him from being sent to a *Children's Home*. Without her, everything that was safe and familiar would begin to fall apart. Already he was cold and empty on the inside. He could almost believe that the world beyond his bedroom door had already begun to crumble away, to vanish like used-up magic now that she who created it was on her way to join the angels in heaven.

When he tried to eat, the stolen food stuck in his throat to remind him of his wickedness. He drank lemonade until his belly became bloated with wind and the taste came back into his mouth in loud burps. When he slept the most frightening dreams invaded his mind. When he awoke the horror and the sense of loss pinned him to the mattress in helpless distress. There were times when he fancied he could hear familiar sounds coming from downstairs. He recognized Irish Tom's whistle and the deep rumble of his voice, music coming from the best room, the ring of the telephone, the lilt of Smallfry's laughter and that pretty little shriek she always gave when the Irishman tried to tickle her ribs or blow his hot breath into her ear. He heard the tapping of her high-heeled shoes and the man's heavier tread on the hall tiles, the slam of the big front door, their happy excited voices out on the front terrace. He heard all these things and knew that they were only in his imagination, because Smallfry was dead.

Frankie hugged Mr Ted and curled himself up in a tight little ball beneath the army greatcoat. He pushed all memory of the white-shrouded bed and its frail occupant out of his mind, conjuring instead the powerful living beauty of her. There were nights when Buddie had to be away and no friends came to call and the house was very quiet. These were the times he both loved and dreaded, the special occasions he always anticipated with a confusion of excitement and dismay. She would call him downstairs to do her toes, because her unique senses told her that the Bogeyman was restless and Frankie was in great danger. In the hot kitchen he would kneel on a cushion with her feet in his lap and pick at every toenail with the silver file, and she would talk and talk until it became very late and dark. She told him stories about zombies and mass-murderers, werewolves, vampires, beasties and bogeymen. She knew everything there was to know about swamp creatures and blood-sucking insects and innocent-looking plants that ate the flesh of human beings. She was even familiar with leprechauns and gremlins and hideous spiteful trolls that could spirit themselves through locked doors and closed windows. And she knew when the Bogeyman in the room upstairs was hungry for fresh young blood. On these nights she would send him off to bed with his insides churning with fear and his vivid imagination creating something horrendous to lurk in every shadow, every corner of the house. He would wait, trembling and terrified, on the lower steps near the main hall until she went to bed, and if she left the door open he would know, by some unspoken agreement, that it was all right for him to creep into her room.

Her bed was always warm despite the coolness of its crisp white sheets and pillow-cases. He would lie stiffly on the very edge of the mattress, his nostrils filled with the smell of her perfume and his heart pounding with terror of a different, more subtle kind. She never turned out the lamps and always fell asleep almost at once. She would sigh and toss about restlessly, fling back the covers so that her breasts were fully visible through her flimsy nightdress, snuggle close to him until her bottom pressed into his private parts and the heat of her entered his body like fire. He hated those nights when his fear of the dark overcame the special torment of sleeping in her bed. He wanted to touch her. Her closeness made his mouth dry and his head ache. It made him feel excited and happy and dirty and miserable all at the same time. It made him think shameful thoughts about the things men did to women when they went to bed together.

A dry sob rose up from his chest and lodged itself in his throat. He tried to cough it away. Tears sprang to his eyes as he wished, as hard as he knew how to wish, that his father would come home to help Smallfry and stop the men from the orphanage coming to take him away. His troubled mind struggled to devise pictures of the noisy brown-skinned man with the crackling laughter and excessive quicksilver moods. Only that week he had been rushing off to school when Buddie emerged from his pig-swill truck and stopped him in his tracks with a shout of: 'Hey there, soldier, how ya doing?'

Recognizing the playful tone, Frankie had turned and brought himself to attention with a smart salute. Although fearful of being late for school and missing morning assembly, he had waited patiently while Buddie rummaged amongst the cabbage-leaves and carrot-tops and bruised potatoes in the back of his truck. He pulled out a huge red apple which looked firm enough but fell into a soggy mess when he tried to polish it on the front of his shirt. He brushed it to the ground with the backs of his fingers and groped for another. This time he wiped his find more carefully with his khaki handkerchief before tossing it into the boy's cupped hands. The ring in his ear, the heavy chain at his throat and the gold caps on his teeth flashed as he threw back his head and roared with laughter.

'Have yourself a terrific day, soldier,' he said at last, saluting in return.

'Ay, ay, sir.'

'Now git. Go on, *git.*'

'Yes, sir. Thank you, sir.'

Frankie had returned the salute and dashed off, grinning. He arrived at school that morning with only seconds to spare, rushing to join the tail of the class-line as it vanished through the porch and into the assembly-hall. He was proud of his apple. It was green on one side and a brilliant rosy red on the other. Frankie liked apples, but this one had come from the greengrocer who saved all the rubbish from his market-stall in big dustbins for Buddie to collect as food for his pigs. Unlike his careless easy-going father, Frankie was unable to forget its unsavoury origins. At playtime he swapped it to Ronnie McEvoy's younger brother for a halfpenny stick of liquorice and seven live matches in a box. He wondered now if the Good Lord and All His Angels punished boys for that kind of disloyalty to a parent.

A noise from beyond the bedroom window pulled his thoughts back to the present. Someone was using an axe outside in the grounds. The rain had stopped, but the wind still gusted beyond the window, throwing the thud of the axe this way and that until the direction of the chopping was impossible to pinpoint. Frankie ventured outside his room and down the stairs a little way. He could see that the door of the best room was shut. He wanted to open it and look inside, or pick up the telephone and dial 999 for help, or even rush outside and yell and yell at the top of his voice until his lungs burst or someone came to take charge of the house and him and his poor dead mother. He knew he should do *something*, but fear was an invisible solid barrier through which he was unable to pass. Instead, he crept back upstairs to the turn of the banister which afforded him the best view of the kitchen door. It was all in darkness, though he felt that some little light should have been visible. It looked to him as if some-one had pulled the heavy curtain and kicked the long mat into place to keep out the draughts. Nobody but Smallfry would do such a thing, and she was lying pale and still on the shrouded bed in the best room.

Frankie chewed nervously on his fingernails. There was definitely someone in the kitchen. Now he must decide whether to go downstairs and confess that his mam was dead because of him, or remain hidden for his own safety. He might even take all his money and dress himself in his warmest clothes and run away to sea where nobody would know his wicked secret. He decided it was too late to do anything but lock himself in his room with his broken chair-leg wedged under the door and hope and pray that the men from the orphanage would not be able to find him in the big dark house. For long hours he seemed to lurch in and out of sleep on a confusing roller-coaster ride that took him from one bad dream to another. When the sound of slamming doors and raised voices finally startled him awake, he was surprised to find himself sitting in a corner of the landing, cold and stiff. One of the voices belonged to Buddie, but it brought the boy no comfort at all because now it occurred to him that Buddie loved Smallfry very, very much and might shoot Frankie with his big shotgun for making her die. The enormity of his guilt came down like a crushing weight on his shoulders. It made him feel sick and broken.

'Frankie! Get down here, boy! At the double!'

He scrambled to his feet and somehow found the strength to propel himself downstairs. The door of the best room was still closed. The door to the kitchen stood open. Buddie was hunched over his meal, glowering angrily. Both dogs were tethered in their usual places beside the stove. Frankie stood in the doorway, blinking in the bright light, head swimming as he stared at Smallfry's favourite chair. She was sitting there in her black costume and slit skirt and shiny patent-leather high-heeled shoes. Her cheeks were pink, her eyes bright, her lips full and crimson as they played in a smile around her perfect teeth. She was sipping tea from her delicate china cup, two fingers hooked prettily, daintily, the way all fine ladies bent their fingers when they drank, as a mark of their breeding.

'Sit down, boy, and eat your food. It's late and you have school in the morning.' Buddie's tone was harsh and unfriendly.

Frankie climbed on to his stool and stared down at his plate. There was a long dark hair lying across his mashed potato. He could see pieces of yellow turnip in his stew. He really hated turnip.

'She'll have to be shot, of course,' Buddie was saying. 'Or sold, maybe. Now she's gotten a taste for it, she'll sure as hell eat every litter she drops in the future. Five pedigree pups, dammit . . . *five* . . . and the stupid animal *eats* every last one of them. My God, I could take an axe to her for what she's done.'

Frankie glanced up at Smallfry. She was dusting something from the lapel of her jacket with the backs of her fingers. Her nails were painted the same vivid glistening crimson as her lips. She was humming very softly to herself. The clock on the wall said a quarter past nine. It was Sunday night. He had been in his room for two days, and the Good Lord and All His Angels had spared Smallfry from her fatal illness and now Frankie felt wrung out and drained and very, very sick.

'What is it, boy? Why do you keep staring at your mam like that? Anyone would think you'd seen a ghost.'

He raised his gaze from the hair in his supper to Smallfry's smiling face. The merest flicker of warning in her eyes, the faintest tightening of her red lips, and he was silenced even before his mind had managed to shape any kind of explanation.

'Don't disobey me, boy,' his father said. 'I'm in no mood to play games. Eat your supper.' His scowl deepened, pulling his dark brows down over his eyes in wrinkled hairy folds. 'What the hell's wrong with him? He looks poorly.'

'Nonsense,' Smallfry smiled. 'He's simply tired. He always looks poorly when he's tired. He was perfectly all right while you were away. Isn't that so, Frankie dear?'

Frankie stared at his food. He tried to remove the hair, only to find that at least half its length was concealed beneath his gravy. His stomach heaved. He could smell stew and tobacco and wet dog-fur and Californian Poppy.

'Eat your supper, Frankie, there's a good boy.'

'Don't talk to him as though he's a damn baby,'

144

Buddie snapped. 'He should eat what's put in front of him. You spoil that kid.'

'But he's my son . . . .'

'He's a snivelling mammy's boy.'

'He's delicate, that's all.'

Buddie's fist rose suddenly and crashed back to the table with such force that Frankie's plate did a little hop to one side. The boy flinched, his face screwing up into nervous contortions. He stared at the long dark hair stretching all the way across his dinner-plate.

'*Delicate*? Delicate my *arse*,' Buddie roared. 'He's just a mummy's boy. It's time someone took him in hand and started to make a man of him. Just look at him. He's twitching like a nervous hound just because he doesn't want to eat his supper and he's scared of getting a thrashing for wasting good food. Get to bed, you ungrateful little mongrel. Get to bed.'

'Oh, Buddie, please don't shout at the poor child . . . '

'*Get to bed*,' Buddie roared, and Frankie, confused and sick inside, almost fell from the high stool before creeping from the room like a whipped animal.

16

FRANKIE FOUND ROSIE'S BODY when he came home from school in the afternoon. She was slumped on the cobbles by the door of the tool-shed, very limp and still. The bulldog was sitting in the farthest top corner of the yard looking very sorry for herself. She was coughing and slavering as if something she had eaten was stuck in her throat and might choke her if it could not be dislodged. He had known something was wrong when the dogs failed to bark as he approached the yard. Now he saw that Rosie was lying motionless, her tongue lolling and a tiny pool of white froth spilled from her mouth. From inside the cobbled arch drifted a heavy unpleasant smell that made him feel nauseous. He stared at Rosie for a long time, waiting for her to breathe. He was quite certain she was dead.

Frankie had not been very well at school. He could not drink his free milk in the morning and had almost fainted when he was sent by Mr Sunderland to help carry the crates and empty bottles out into the yard. Then he had been given fifty lines to write in Mr Dunn's class because he fell asleep with his head on his geography-book and the cuff of his shirt dangling in the inkwell. He was unable to finish his dinner, so he gave his roast potatoes to Wally Watmough and his jam sponge and custard to Denis Taylor. In the afternoon he had tripped and twisted his ankle during agility class, so Mrs Greenwood had insisted that he lie down on one of the little foldaway beds in the rest-room. She promised not to tell a soul that he wet himself in his sleep, but she wrote a note to his mam saying that he should be kept at home for a few days and taken to the school clinic in Edmund Street for a check-up. He did not know what was wrong with him. He was worn out and listless. He could neither concentrate on anything nor force his body to do what he wanted it to do. He was very late getting home because he had to walk so slowly that the other boys were already out of sight before he turned the corner from Longside Lane into Shearbridge Road. He trudged all the way home with his head lowered and his hands in his pockets, thinking of nothing.

He could see Smallfry in the grounds when he squeezed through the gate at the side of Brooke Parker's. She was down beyond the front terrace, not on the slopes but to one side where the land was flat enough for the pigs to be housed and where she rarely ventured because of the mud and the stink. She was wearing a pair of Buddie's working pants which she had cut down and sewn on her treadle machine, only they did not seem to fit her properly. They were too tight across her backside. They showed every wobble of her flesh when she walked, and the centre stitching appeared to separate her buttocks in a way that made all the men stare. She also wore one of Buddie's brightly coloured shirts with the sleeves rolled to her elbows, the collar standing stiffly up into her hair and the bottom knotted below her breasts so that the middle part of her body was bare. She looked like Rita Hayworth, except that her hair was tied up in a pony-tail and held in place with a bow of blue ribbon. She was laughing. She looked very young, not like a mother at all. As Frankie watched from the gate, Tom Fish scooped her into his arms and swung her over the muddy patch near the pig-pens. Then they walked together towards the little brick house where Adam had once lived.

Adam was the goose. Buddie used to say that he was the biggest and most cantankerous goose ever to be hatched from a single egg. He would bite anyone and everyone who crossed his path, chasing them around the grounds and nipping at their legs and ankles with a beak capable of drawing blood or leaving a nasty bruise that would hurt for days. All the other animals avoided him. Even Rosie kept her distance and simply barked hysterically whenever the ill-tempered gander was around. Everyone feared him, but Buddie laughed at his vicious antics and called him the best goddam guard-dog in the world. He did not seem to mind that the hateful animal savaged his hands and legs each time he approached the pen with its food. Then one day Adam cornered Smallfry on the front terrace and attacked her so fiercely that her screams could be heard as far away as Thorpe Street and her legs had to be painted with iodine and bandaged from knee to ankle for a fortnight. Buddie had caught Adam by the throat and sliced off his head with a big meat-knife even before the doctor arrived in answer to his urgent call, and that weekend there was roast goose with orange stuffing and baked potatoes for Sunday dinner.

After the old gander was eaten and his bones burned in the stove, the little brick house where he had lived was cleaned out and converted into a storage-place for papers and tarpaulins and other things that needed to be kept dry. Long ago, Frankie had tried to peep inside the locked building by rubbing the thick glass in the window with his hand to clear away years of accumulated dirt. He had not realized that the glass ended a little way short of the top of the frame, leaving a gap of about an inch into which his fingers slipped. He was rubbing and polishing quite firmly when the first finger

148

of his right hand skimmed along its rough upper edge and burst open in a gaping bloody wound. Even now he could see the round black scar that sat just off-centre from the whirls of his fingerprint and served as a reminder that little boys should never pry into things that do not concern them. As he watched his mam and the Irishman disappear through the door of Adam the Gander's little brick house, he tried not to think of other things that were also none of his business.

Frankie had walked along the back drive, past the yard of the first house where grass now grew in tall clumps between the paving stones and a trio of bright dandelions sprouted from a corner of the back door-step. At the tiny pantry window he had paused to listen, expecting to hear the sound of chains dragging across the yard and Rosie's growls gathering in the back of her throat. All he heard was the bulldog's weary coughing and a loud hissing sound coming from the tool-shed. It took him a long time to summon sufficient courage to cross the yard and approach the spot where the body of the Great Dane lay. She looked much smaller, lying on the cobbles with her eyes glazed and staring and all the meanness gone out of her. Frankie stood there until his stomach began to heave and his head to swim. The hissing noise was coming from the shattered lead pipe in the corner of the tool-shed. Rosie had died because she had bitten into the pipe just as she chewed through everything that came within her reach. She had gassed herself, and the sickening smell and the hissing sound were indications that the deadly gas was still pouring freely from the fracture.

The back door was locked. Frankie began to cough as he ran to unhook Lady's chain and drag the reluctant bulldog from the yard. Despite his efforts to take her right away, she broke free in the drive and flopped

149

down beside one of the turkey-pens, panting and retching. He left her there and ran round the house to the front terrace, where he limped, rasping and damp-eyed, along the crazy paving. The sound of music told him that Buddie was sitting on the front steps, plucking and strumming at his guitar. Frankie glanced at the trees at the far end of the terrace. They were all in full leaf. Neither the pigsties nor the little brick house beyond them could be seen from the terrace or the wide front steps of the house.

'Buddie! Buddie! Come quick!'

'What is it, boy? What's wrong?'

'It's Rosie,' he said breathlessly. 'She's bitten the gas-pipe and now she's dead and Lady's poorly and the gas is leaking all over the yard.'

'Jesus Christ!'

Buddie leaped to his feet and dashed into the house, shouting and cursing as he made for the back door. Frankie wanted to follow him and offer his help, but the effort of dragging Lady from the yard and running to raise the alarm had exhausted him. He sat down on the bottom step in the hall and allowed his head to slump between his knees. He did not know how long he had been sitting there when Buddie shook him by the shoulder.

'Here, Frankie, drink this. It'll settle your stomach and make you feel better.'

The milk in the cup was warm and sweet. Frankie drank gratefully. He was glad when Buddie sat down on the step beside him.

'Rosie's dead. She gassed herself.'

'Yes, I know,' Frankie offered.

'Was it you who let Lady out of the yard?'

Frankie nodded. 'She didn't want to come, but I made her. Will she be all right?'

'I reckon so. You did well, Frankie. Where's your mam?'

Frankie lowered his head and stared at the milk in his cup.

'I don't know,' he muttered.

'Hey, are you feeling all right?' Buddie placed his rough palm on the boy's chin, lifted his face and scowled into his eyes. 'Did you sniff the gas? Are you feeling sick?'

Frankie tried to tell his father that he was perfectly all right, but something happened to spill his milk and the next thing he knew he was undressed and tucked up in Smallfry's bed with Dr Thambi standing over him. Dr Thambi was black. He had cold hands and tight woolly hair, gold-rimmed glasses and a shiny solemn face that reminded Frankie of the sad old gorilla pictured in one of Buddie's *National Geographic* magazines. He liked Dr Thambi's gravel-rough voice, his small tilted-back ears and his clean comforting smell.

Smallfry rushed into the room in a panic, demanding to see her son at once. When she spotted Frankie lying in the big bed she gave a choked cry of alarm and threw up her arms, dropping the flowers she had collected and swaying as if she might faint from shock. Then she perched herself on the edge of the bed and stroked his face and patted his hand. The pretty ribbon had gone from her hair, and her lipstick was smudged at one side of her mouth. She blinked her eyes and worked her mouth as ladies were expected to do when bravely trying not to break down and cry.

'Oh, my poor baby,' she said in a half-sob. 'My poor, poor baby. He might have died. I was down there in the garden . . . all alone . . . never suspecting that my son . . . my little boy . . . .'

151

As Buddie took her by the arm and led her away, her hands came up to cover her face and her shoulders began to shake. She was crying because her little boy was ill and had to be looked at by the doctor. Frankie hated to upset her, especially when she herself might sicken and die at any moment, but somehow her concern made him feel warm inside and not at all sorry that he was so poorly.

He was given Fenning's Fever Cure on a tablespoon. It was the most horrible medicine he had ever tasted, but it was quickly followed by a spoonful of delicious malt-and-cod-liver oil from the thick brown jar in Buddie's cupboard. He licked the spoon clean, then savoured the lingering sweetness adhering to the back of his throat. He was sorry Rosie had killed herself, even though she had eaten her pups and bitten him several times and terrorized him for years. At the same time he was happy that Lady was going to be all right once the gas had gone from her lungs. She was an old dog who only made trouble when she tried to follow Rosie's example. She had produced lots of fine bulldog puppies in the past for selling, and once she had barked and barked in the night until Buddie got out of bed to find two men with crowbars trying to break open the door of the chicken-house. The sight of the shotgun and the fierce-looking bulldog loosed from its chain sent them scuttling away, and that's when Buddie had decided to buy Adam the Gander, the best goddam guard-dog in the world until Rosie came.

Buddie was sitting on the wooden fender, strumming his guitar and humming to himself. The big silver ring on his little finger seemed to twinkle in the firelight, releasing the flashes of colour trapped in its seemingly transparent stone. Frankie began to drift into sleep, cushioned between soft white sheets, lulled by the perfumed warmth of his mother's bed. He was so glad he had saved Lady's life by pulling her away from the gas. He had a feeling Buddie was proud of him for what he had done.

They woke him in the evening to move him into the music-room where a bed had been made up and a small coal-fire set in the grate. His bed was meant for only one person. It had a dip in the middle where the flock mattress was worn and the wires below had sagged under the weight of many occupants. The pillow was also stuffed with flock that had to be kneaded, like the mattress, to smooth out the hard lumps and make it more comfortable. There was only one large sheet, which was frayed at the edges and folded in two beneath the blankets. Someone had opened the shutters halfway across the window so that he could see reflections of the room on the glass. Outside on the terrace, the trees made leafy black patterns in silhouette against the darkening sky. There was porridge for supper with lashings of hot milk and sweet sticky treacle that ran in golden swirls from his spoon. Smallfry was wonderful. She smiled at him all the time and tested his forehead for fever and looked very sad when she had to leave him alone again. Nanny had sent him some striped pyjamas from Lansdowne Place because his own, which he could not remember owning, were in the wash. He liked the way the sleeves hung down past his fingertips and the legs covered his toes so that he was warm all over. There was a rubber sheet, too, because sick children sometimes had night accidents and his nanny did not want him to be sleeping in a wet bed. Sickness had always frightened Frankie, but now that his head had stopped aching and his stomach churning he felt that he might enjoy being an invalid for a few days.

He lay back with his hands clasped behind his

153

head and his knees raised up to create a mound of his bedclothes. Flickering fire-shapes danced across the ceiling, chasing back the darker shadows. He could see the caricatures and Walt Disney characters Buddie had drawn on big sheets of white paper and pinned to the walls above the wooden picture-rail. He liked Mickey Mouse and Minnie and Goofy the dog, but most of all he liked the comic drawings of real living people. There was noisy Blossom, all bushy hair and mouth and teeth, drawn with a huge grinning face, pudding breasts and a little stick body like a pipe-cleaner doll's. There, too, was Sammy Peacock, with his smiley mouth and huge bony nose; and Chas Johnson the drummer, as swarthy as a tinker with wavy black hair that curled around his collar and sometimes hung forward over his eyes. Marching across the opposite wall was poor Tommy Crowley, whose hollow cheeks, deep-set eyes and long protruding chin might have been caused by the consumption that was slowly killing him. And there was his brother Charlie, who looked just like Stan Laurel and had lived for years in Nanny's house and was married to one of Frankie's aunts so that she could claim his army pension.

He stared sleepily at the pictures of Buddie drawn by Miss Claydon at the School of Art. She was what Buddie called a true artist. She could make him look like a Cherokee warrior or a proud gypsy, an Arab or an Indian prince, a Greek or a Spaniard, yet never really like anyone else but Buddie. She could even make his black eyes follow Frankie around the room as if watching and judging his every move.

The door of the music-room opened and a shadow appeared in the gap. For an instant his heart leaped, then he remembered that the Bogeyman never left his room when Buddie was in the house and never, ever entered any of the lower rooms. He smiled as the door closed again very gently. Someone was checking to see that he was all right. He could turn over and snuggle down in his clean new bed and know that he was safe in his parents' care.

17

It WAS TO BE four whole days and nights before the nice clean bed with the real sheet was removed from the music-room and he was unceremoniously ordered back to his old bedroom on the first floor. Nanny had sent him a tin of sweets and some comics, and Buddie had loaned him his special pencils and a whole stack of paper on which to draw pictures. Frankie was good at drawing. It was one of the few subjects he could actually face with confidence at school. He had also been given a book, a thick book with a coloured cover and a story inside about three brave brothers and their fantastic adventures in a foreign country. He was allowed to keep the shutters back all day and only partly closed at night. This meant that his new room was never really dark, never thick and heavy with a blackness that pressed like damp blankets over his face until his heart swelled and threatened to choke him from the inside. He wanted to stay there for ever, because in the downstairs room there was no Bogeyman, and he could forget that he was frightened of the dark.

Buddie came into the music-room every day to practise his guitar or read his newspaper. He did not always speak to the boy, and sometimes the scowl was so deeply etched into his brow that Frankie hardly dare move for fear of disturbing him; but he was there, and it was sharing of a kind.

There was a letter on the mantlepiece that had come

from his other nanny in Park Road. She wanted him to get better soon so that he could go to visit her and she would make a cake with caraway seeds especially for him. She told him that Peter the budgie had escaped from his cage and flown round and round the room until she caught him in a towel and put him back to stop him flying away when the door was opened. There was a postal order in the envelope. If Frankie took it to the post office, the man behind the counter would change it for two shillings and sixpence, which was the same as half a crown.

Frankie did a great deal of thinking while he was poorly and lying quietly in his bed for all those long comfortable hours. He had come to the conclusion that not every grown-up was perfect after all. His other nanny was a grown-up, and she did not even know that her seedcake was dry and horrible and that the taste of caraway seeds, especially when they became fast in the cracks between his teeth, always made him feel sick. At school the grown-ups were so clever that they knew everything about *everything*, but still Mrs Craven ate chalk, which was very bad for her, and even Mr Sunderland, the headmaster, picked his nose and rolled what he found between his fingers before smearing it on the side of his desk. They were not all perfect. Some of the men who worked around Old Ashfield took things that did not belong to them and used bad language and did dirty things with the ladies who came to visit them. Irish Tom was the worst of all, and Frankie hated him. He was mean and spiteful. He liked to invent games in which Frankie got hurt or had to run away and cry because he was made to look such a fool in front of everyone. Sooner or later, the worst kids at school were found out and chastised or sent away for what they did to other children, but nobody

157

ever punished adults, and sometimes they could be the most cruel bullies of all.

His days off school had not all been easy. Smallfry had smacked his face for telling lies when Buddie became very angry about his wet sheet. Twice he confessed that he had wet the bed, and twice she promised to change the sheet, but when Buddie found it she denied all knowledge of his accidents. Smallfry never really lied, because she hated and despised all liars, but she must have forgotten about Frankie's complaints because she slapped him very hard, right there in front of Buddie, and made him confess to being a liar even though he knew he was telling the truth. She said she would have changed the sheet immediately, if only she had known it was wet and smelly, but Frankie had told her about it: he had, he had, he *had*.

On another day Smallfry suddenly announced that his daily spoonful of Buddie's delicious malt-and-cod-liver oil was to be discontinued because it made him violently sick. If Frankie could not recall being sick all over his new bed, then he was either too ill to remember or too dishonest to tell the truth to his father. Frankie always forgave her when she made mistakes. Life was very difficult for her, and she bore the secret of her terrible illness much more bravely than even Bette Davis or Joan Crawford could have done. Sometimes she would sit beside his bed and recite the wonderful long poems she had memorized from special books, and even Buddie would stare at her and listen to her every word as the heroine died for love or the highwayman came riding, riding by. It was sometimes so easy to look at her and love her and forget that she was dying.

On the last day of his convalescence she sat with him for a long time, holding his hand while she broke the awful news with tears in her eyes and a pretty tremble on her lower lip. She begged him, as her loyal and loving son, to keep it their special secret, at least for a little while. Frankie had nodded numbly, too stunned by her words to speak out loud.

He had learned a long time ago that nothing in life ever stayed the same. Things changed. Sunny days faded away long before he was ready to let them go. Dark nights vanished while his eyes were closed. Sooner or later nice kids were turned into class monitors or moved up to the Big School where they became neither friend nor enemy, just different. Even things that hurt worse than anything at the time would eventually change, like the dog-bite on his leg that healed of its own accord until he could not even recall what it felt like to be in all that pain. When the holidays came and school closed down until September, he would be convinced that summer, with its long days and short nights, would last for ever, until it, too, changed. The end of summer was a whole lifetime away, yet in no time at all he would be ten, then eleven, then the newest and smallest and thinnest kid at the Big School, and he was dreading it. Everything changed. It might take a long time or hardly any time at all, and sometimes the biggest change of all took just a few words whispered in confidence between a boy and his mam.

Dr Thambi had spoken to him about his height. He told him that there were children in Africa who started out small and grew to be Watutsi or Masai or Dinka warriors who were all remarkably tall and fierce and were feared and respected by the men of other tribes. Dr Thambi was himself a big man. He had a thick muscular neck and very wide shoulders, and even in his smart suits, waistcoats and stiff white collars he looked like a weight-lifter or a tough prize-fighter. He, too, had seen the tiny little man with the short legs

159

and arms who lived in Horton Grange Road; the man with the big grown-up's head on a small child's body. Frankie's question had caused the doctor to shake his head gravely.

'Let me assure you that you are not a dwarf, Frankie,' he said. 'You are simply not tall, just as nobody in your family is particularly tall, but you are certainly not a dwarf.'

Frankie hung his head, unconvinced. Smallfry knew best. Only that morning she had fallen into a rage and called him a nigger and a dwarf because something had happened to make her very angry. There was a red mark on her cheek and a small bruise near her mouth. He had seen her arguing with the Irishman and wondered if Big Tom Fish, with his huge callused hands, had dared to strike her in the face. If this were so, Frankie knew that one day he would kill him for it.

Two men in dark suits, both with stern unfriendly faces and large-rimmed hats, had come to the house to speak to the man in the attic. Frankie was still standing in the hall with his face in a corner and his hands on his head because Smallfry had forgotten to let him out of disgrace. He peeped sideways under his arms as the two men passed him on their way to the stairs. They looked like detectives, except that their accents were strange and their manners overly polite. After a while they went away muttering to themselves and scribbling in matching notebooks. Later, the man came down from the attic and spent a long time alone in the bathroom. He was barely recognizable with his beard shaved off and his hair cut short around his ears. To Frankie's amazement the man had been invited to sit at the table with them at tea-time. Buddie spoke a few words to him in Polish, which must have been his own language because his English was very poor. Frankie had not really liked him. He was strange and quiet and watchful, and he stared at Smallfry all the time and coughed without covering his mouth with his hand. Now the attic door was to remain unlocked, and the man who had lived up there above Frankie's room for so long would soon be taken away to be cared for by his own people. More changes. It worried Frankie when things that were quite momentous in his life took place as if they were not really important at all.

Frankie had made himself some stilts out of upturned soup-tins and lengths of stout string. First he filled the empty tins with lumps of brick to prevent them collapsing under the strain, then he hammered a small hole in each side through which to thread the string. He knotted it tightly and made the loops long enough to grip in each hand when he was standing on the tins. By yanking and jerking these makeshift handles with every stride, he was able to make forward progress in a lurching gait so long as he kept the tin cans firmly beneath his feet. In this way he hobbled along the rear driveway and up the long slope to the top of Thorpe Street. By the time he reached the concrete loading-ramp outside the doors of Brooke Parker's, the muscles in his legs were aching and the rough string had worn a tender ridge across his fingers.

He left his stilts out of sight by the wall and looked down the long deserted street. None of the local kids was playing outside. A fine rain was falling, and the heavy grey sky made it seem much later than six-thirty in the evening. He had tuppence in his pocket. If he hurried, he could catch Mrs Bland before she locked up her cluttered little shop on the corner at the bottom of the street. Mrs Bland sold crunchy peanut butter from a huge bin on the counter. With her bone-handled knife she lifted great dollops of the sticky treat and transferred it to sheets of greaseproof paper laid across the scales. For tuppence Frankie could buy enough

161

peanut butter to cover four slices of bread generously, but he usually ate it straight from the paper, scooping it into his mouth by the fingerful.

He turned up his collar against the fine drizzle of rain and prepared to run down the left-hand side of the street, leaping every cobbled passage-space as he went. There were twelve passages on that side, each one leading to the outside lavatories of four back-to-back houses. He slipped into the first passage to pee against the wall in the very spot where Jimmy Hobson's dad had kept his old bike until the gypsies came in the night and stole it away. He could see the tiny windows that drew a meagre amount of daylight into the cellar-head kitchens of each house, and below them the metal coal-hole covers that slid upward to reveal holes in the walls so that coalmen could tip their heavy sacks directly into the cellars. George Augustus boasted that he was going to be a real coalman when he grew up, just like his father and his two uncles before him. He was already bigger and stronger than any other boy of his age, and Frankie sometimes wondered if growing tall was all just a matter of what a boy intended to be in life. He was not sure that he particularly wanted to be *anything* when he grew up, unless he could join a circus or be a cowboy in America. If he went on saving and hiding his money, he would be a millionaire, and perhaps he did not need to be very tall or strong in order to live his life as a wealthy man.

As he emerged from the passage he remembered old Mrs Barraclough, who was very fat and had lived in Thorpe Street since before even Buddie was born. Mrs Barraclough's husband had been one of those unfortunate people who died in the war without ever being a soldier. She called him a poor unsung hero and cried shame on the Government for not recognizing men like him so that their names could be added to those on the

162

war memorials. He had died for his country. He had made the greatest sacrifice of all, and not a soul apart from old Mrs Barraclough cared that he was gone.

The Barracloughs' cellar had a window at ground-level and a deep well cut away so that light and air could reach it. The well had originally been covered by a grid made of iron railings which the Barracloughs generously contributed to the war effort. A large plank of wood had been laid across the well in its place, and Mrs Barraclough always said that anyone actually stepping on the plank should not be passing so close to her sitting-room window anyway, because the pavement was wide enough for them to walk on the flags. Paddy O'Donnell did not know about the Barracloughs' cellar-well. He fell over the plank one dark night while staggering home, dead drunk, from a drinking club in Morley Street. He broke both legs, one wrist, two fingers, his nose and the cellar window in the fall. When poor Mr Barraclough rushed downstairs to investigate the commotion in his cellar, he found a muddy figure sprawled upside-down across the stone sink, bleeding profusely and singing 'Carry Me Back to Bonny Dublin' into Mrs Barraclough's bread-crock. The shock was too much for the old man. He muttered something about a foreign invasion, clutched at his chest with both hands and dropped down dead on the spot. Mrs Barraclough had always blamed the Government. They were happy enough to take the railings to help the war effort. They should be made to pay compensation, because a new window had to be paid for, poor Mr Barraclough was struck down in the prime of his life and Paddy O'Donnell spent three months in traction for want of a cellar-grate.

Frankie felt very sorry for Mrs Barraclough. He thought she kept the nicest outside lavatory in Thorpe Street. It was down at the end of the passage, and she

163

cut her newspaper into neat squares before threading it
on to a loop of wire which hooked over the pipe where it
bent out from the cistern tank. This made the paper
easy to pull free and allowed it to hang in mid-air so that
it stayed clean and dry. Mrs Smith, who had the
lavatory next door, pushed bits of paper behind the pipe
near the back of the pot where it became damp and
spiders could crawl all over it. Hers was a bare stone
place with a dripping cistern and cobwebs in every
corner and a funny smell in the pot. Mrs Barraclough's
lavatory had a square of real linoleum on the floor and
whitewashed walls that left chalky stains on anything
that brushed against them. She even scrubbed and
yellow-stoned the little doorstep, just like her front
step and window-ledge. Mrs Barraclough deserved
compensation from the Government, if not for her dead
husband then certainly for her nice clean lavatory.

Frankie prepared himself for his run, pushed off
with his left leg and raced down the street like a bullet,
leaping every passage-space and not allowing his feet
to touch a single cobble. He made eight enormous
strides and then soared through the air in a leap,
working up a rhythm worthy of any athlete. He felt
sure that if he jumped all twelve spaces without
making a mistake he would reach Mrs Bland's place in
time to buy his peanut butter. At last he arrived at the
corner shop, convinced of his success, only to find the
shop-door locked and the leather blind pulled down
over the side-window. Feeling cheated and let down,
he seated himself on the step to recover his breath and
stared into the curtain of rain falling across Shearbridge Road.

Last summer he had tried his best to fly, because
Buddie told him he could do it for sure if he took a long
hard downhill run at it. So Frankie had practised
every day by running flat out all the way down Thorpe

164

Street and leaping into the air with his arms waving like frantic wings when he reached the bottom. He had tried for weeks on end without success. Then one day he miscalculated on his final leap and found himself hurtling helplessly out into Shearbridge Road to land in the path of an oncoming brewery-lorry. The lorry had screeched to a halt only inches from where he lay sprawled in the road with skinned knees and hands and a bloody nose. A man called John Delany, who owned an enormous scrap-metal yard on the other side of the road, had picked him up by the scruff of his neck and shaken him until his teeth rattled for being a very stupid little boy and hurling himself into a busy main road as if determined to kill himself. John Delany said if people were meant to fly they would be born with wings instead of with arms. Frankie had immediately abandoned his attempts to take to the air by racing down Thorpe Street and leaping from the ground with his arms flapping. When he jumped the passage-spaces he always stopped long before he reached the main road. He was afraid of being run over by a brewery-lorry, and he was scared that John Delany would tell Buddie how carelessly he had carried out his instructions.

18

HE HAD NOT EXPECTED Smallfry to be waiting for him when he got home. She called out to him in a very loud voice as he squeezed through the gap below the safety-chain and closed the front door quietly behind him.

'Come here, you!'

His heart seemed to dip and roll before swelling into his throat. He knew the tone of her voice only too well. She was angry in that calm deliberate way which frightened him even more than her screaming rages, because these angers made her cruel and might take days to burn themselves out. The kitchen door was wide open. She was sitting in the bright light at the end of the dark corridor, her legs crossed at the knee and her foot jigging up and down the way it always did when she was really cross. Frankie suddenly realized that his clothes were wet and he was trailing mud through the house with every step. He prayed she would not notice his dirty hands and scuffed shoes. His hands were trembling as he hastily straightened his collar and smoothed down his hair. He had not expected her to be waiting for him. Not knowing what wicked thing he might have done to make her so annoyed, he walked down the corridor with his heart pounding.

'Come here! Where have you been since tea-time?'

'Playing out, Smallfry.' He stepped into the hot kitchen and lowered his head so that she would not accuse him of dumb insolence for staring at her.

'Where? Where were you playing?'

'In Thorpe Street, Smallfry.'

'With whom?'

'Nobody. There was nobody to play with.'

'Who knows about the secret? Who have you told it to?'

He looked up, eyes wide with protest.

'Nobody! I didn't tell . . . honest . . . I didn't tell.'

She reached into a dish on the table and took out a piece of green soap that had been softening in warm water. Frankie groaned inwardly.

'Go upstairs and get ready for bed,' she told him. 'I want you back here in five minutes.'

Frankie hurried upstairs. A narrow band of light was showing along the bottom of the Bogeyman's door. He crept past it with his back against the banister, holding his breath, and when he reached his own room he was shivering. His mind was racing, but he could not remember anything happening since tea-time to put her in one of those moods. He had not breathed a word about the merchant navy to any living soul, but Smallfry obviously did not trust him to keep her secret. Now she was going to give him a soap suppository, and that was something he dreaded almost as much as the worm-cakes that tore at his insides and left a nasty taste in his mouth for days.

He returned to the kitchen a few minutes later wearing his pyjamas and carrying his wet clothes in a bundle. He put the clothes on the floor by the fire and stood before her while her painted fingers shaped the softened soap into a long bullet-shaped pellet. The room was very hot. He could smell the dampness of his clothes as they began to steam in the heat. He watched her fingers working the soap. The waiting was all part of his ordeal.

'Come here, you.'

167

He stepped forward, not looking at her.

'Trousers.'

His fingers fumbled over the rubber button fastening his pyjama pants. At last the pants slipped to the floor in a heaped figure of eight and he stepped out of them. He was trembling.

'Bend over.'

Frankie dangled himself over her bent knees, a compliant helpless conspirator in his own humiliation. He felt her eyes and her fingers probing his buttocks, felt the pellet of soap slide into his body and her hands massaging his flesh to work it home.

'Now stand over there.'

He obeyed without question. He wiped the tears from his eyes with the sleeve of his pyjama jacket, then gripped the front flaps and held them firmly over his genitals, blessing Nanny for sending something large enough to cover his shame. His vest would have been inches too short, and he hated it when Smallfry looked at his private parts. He always felt that she was judging and measuring with her eyes and despising him for what she saw.

The clock on the wall ticked loudly in the quiet room. Lady heaved herself from her alcove by the stove and waddled across to a cooler spot by the back door. She flopped down with her chin on her front paws and emitted a number of wet sighs. Her wrinkled face was doleful, her dark eyes brimming with perpetual tears. She looked ugly and sad, a docile old lady now that her more adventurous companion had deserted her. She had neither barked nor snarled at anyone since the day Rosie gassed herself in the tool-shed.

Frankie tightened his buttocks and stood very still. Smallfry was touching the edges of her fingernails with a silver file. Her lips were pursed, and from time to time she smiled, or frowned, or sucked in her cheeks

168

and lifted one eyebrow as if her face was acting out her private thoughts.

'Please, Smallfry . . . I have to go.'

'Not until I say so.'

He held his breath. The long hand on the clock jerked slightly to mark the passing of another minute.

'Please, Smallfry . . . . '

'Don't snivel, Frankie. You know I can't *bear* it when you snivel. And stop all that dancing about. *Stop it.*'

'I can't . . . . I need to go . . . . '

She sighed and examined her fingers more closely.

'Please . . . Smallfry . . . *please* . . . . '

At last she extended her hand and waved her fingers in a small gesture of dismissal. He grabbed his pyjama pants and ran, only to be halted at the door by her harsh voice.

'Don't you *dare* leave that stinking pile of rags in my kitchen.'

He dashed back, scooped up his clothes, hugged them against his chest and rushed from the room. Her voice brought him to a skidding halt just as he reached the main staircase. With a sob he limped back to the kitchen, his buttocks nipped tightly together and his feet shuffling in tiny steps.

'Haven't you forgotten something?'

'Yes, Smallfry.'

'Well?'

He limped across the room, wiped the back of his hand across his mouth and stretched up to kiss her turned cheek. Her brows arched haughtily over her lowered lids and her mouth pulled down at the corners as if his touch filled her with distaste.

'You may go,' she said coldly, and once again he turned on his heels and dashed from the room.

To his utter relief his prayers were answered and he reached the bathroom with seconds to spare. There had been times in the past when he had not been so fortunate, and she had screamed at him and called him nasty names and made him clean up the mess with newspaper and a wet cloth. He really hated the suppositories, even though he knew they were for his own good. They helped prevent spots and bad teeth and cleared away all his inner impurities so that constipation would not make him ill. He knew all this, but still he hated the suppositories.

Morning came warm and sunny, with birds chattering in the trees outside his window and stains of bright sunshine touching the wall near the edges of his blackout blanket. It was a beautiful day. Everything outside looked clean and fresh after yesterday afternoon's rain. Today he was going to his other nanny's house in Park Road, to thank her for the postal order and stay with her for a whole afternoon while Smallfry went somewhere to visit a friend. He liked his nanny. Not even the promise of a huge slice of her caraway cake could spoil the pleasure of a trip to her house.

Frankie had left his trousers and bomber jacket draped over the hot-water tank in the cistern cupboard, his shoes wedged down the side of the tank and his socks and shirt wound around the warmest pipe. As he had hoped, the heat of the tank, maintained throughout the night by the fire in the stove in the kitchen, had dried his clothes sufficiently for him to put them on without shivering or feeling clammy beneath their dampness. His new leather shoes were baked stiff and dry, with chalky white stains here and there which refused to budge in spite of his rubbing furiously at them with a corner of his blanket. Hoping that the worst creases in his clothes would eventually be smoothed away by the warmth of his body, he combed his hair with the metal nit-comb and settled

170

himself at the turn of the banister to watch the kitchen door and wait for someone to call him downstairs.

He could tell by the tone of her voice that she was still angry when at last she stood at the kitchen door and called his name. She was wearing one of her lovely swing-backed coats: the checked one with the patch pockets and high collar and a belt that appeared through side-slits and knotted at the front, leaving the back of the coat full and loose. Buddie offered to take them in the jeep, but Smallfry shook her head with her lips pressed tightly together. She preferred to walk because the fresh air would be good for Frankie.

He had to kneel on the floor to check that the seams in her stockings were perfectly straight. She was wearing the peep-toed shoes with the coloured wedges, and he knew that the handbag hung over her arm was made from genuine snake-skin. Her hair was brushed into a pony-tail and held with a black velvet bow. She had smeared a little soap on to her dampened hands and smoothed the hairs at the nape of her neck so that not a single hair hung out of place. Earlier in the week, Frankie had watched her make those particular ear-rings by covering plain clips with snippets of fabric cut from the inner facings of her coat. He knew there was not another woman in Bradford whose jewellery so exactly matched her clothes. She was clever and she was beautiful, and she made him feel very, very proud.

She forgot to give Frankie his breakfast. It was ten minutes past eleven when they left the house, and by this time his stomach was groaning and rumbling with hunger. As he walked behind her along the rear driveway towards the gate, he watched her hair shimmering in the sunlight and forgave her the oversight. She was not like other mothers. Life was easy for all those other women because they did not know anything better. They were dull and unintelligent, with no

171

ambition and no hope of being elevated to a better life. Smallfry was different. She was special. She belonged in a finer place, like fabulous London or glittering Hollywood. She only stayed in Bradford to take care of Frankie so that he would not be put in a *Home*. Her sacrifice was his gain. He would not be an ungrateful child and break her heart by complaining just because she forgot to give him some breakfast.

Nanny's house was warm and clean, with lots of dark colours and shiny polished furniture. She was glad to see him. She kissed him and looked very closely into his face, making little tut-tutting sounds with her tongue that were somehow friendly and not at all critical. He had to sit quietly on the chaise-longue while Smallfry and Nanny stood together in the tiny kitchen at the head of the cellar stairs, talking in hushed voices while they waited for the kettle to boil. They were discussing the *secret*. He tried not to listen, and not to think about the frightening thing Smallfry had told him, because then the fluttering in his stomach would turn to panic and he would let her down and anger her by his snivelling.

He always felt happy in this nanny's house. He liked the way the spiky horse-hairs from the frayed edge of the sofa penetrated the fabric of his pants to prick at his skin like little hot needles. He liked the trio of pot geese on the big sideboard, each facing in a different direction because their smooth bases slipped on the polished surface. He enjoyed sniffing at the big oval bar of coal-tar soap, so good for Nanny's scaly forearms, that left sticky marks on the sink and a distinctive smell in the air. Nanny polished her rosewood sideboard until the wood shone and the brass fittings glistened like pure gold. On either side of it hung her rare and precious glass-paintings: two tall narrow mirrors in heavy wooden frames, each bearing a painting beautifully

172

done in oils. One was called 'Stag at Bay'. It showed a magnificent great-horned stag on a misty Scottish hillside, rounding bravely on the fierce deer-hound snapping at its heels. The other picture showed the same animal standing guard beneath a darkening sky, master of the wild moorland landscape. This one was aptly entitled 'Monarch of the Glen'. Frankie never tired of looking into those wonderfully detailed paintings. When he touched the rough brush-strokes the bracken and heather sprang to life beneath his finger-tips and the flanks of the stag felt coarse and warm and very real. He had always known that one day, when he was grown up and very rich, he would buy a house of his own that had exactly the same glass-paintings hanging on its sitting-room walls.

He shuffled his bottom this way and that until the horse-hairs pricked the tender skin on the backs of his knees. As always, Peter the budgie was chirruping tirelessly in his cage by the window. Frankie listened very carefully but, no matter how hard he tried, he could not imagine that those funny little noises resembled real words.

There was a tea-tray on the table with pretty plates and a whole stack of currant tea-cakes piled into a basket. He guessed his nanny would slice them in half and toast them on the end of her long brass fork so that the butter would melt and make his fingers deliciously sticky. He had decided never to let Nanny know that her caraway cake made him feel sick, because then things would change and Frankie wanted everything to remain the same for ever. He wanted to feel the horse-hair scratching his skin and hide his caraway seeds in the tab rug and wash his hands in coal-tar soap for the rest of his life. Most of all he wanted his nanny to stay the same. He did not want her to grow old and die of a stroke like Alan Turner's granny, who

173

had to be given flowers every first Sunday in the month even though she was dead and buried in the ground at Scholemoor cemetery.

Smallfry hurried out without letting him kiss her goodbye. He rushed to the door to watch her walk along Park Lane but, although he called and called her name in his mind, she did not turn to look back before vanishing round the corner into Little Horton Lane.

Nanny was happy because Buddie had sent her some best butter and a dozen fresh eggs and a whole chicken, just for herself. She was wearing neither her thick trousers nor her head-scarf tied in a turban, because today was Saturday and she did not have to go to work at the brewery down Manchester Road. Her hair was thinning at the crown and turning from brown to white because she was quite old and had a lot of wrinkles. She had fastened three rows of curling-pins all the way round her head so that her hair would look nice when she went to the pub to drink beer or to the club to play cards. When she pulled out the pins her hair would spring back into tight little sausages that turned to frizzy curls when they were brushed.

Nanny had very thick, discoloured fingernails, and some of her fingers had turned brown because she smoked Woodbine cigarettes from slender green packets which she kept in her handbag and in the sideboard cupboard with her gin. Her hands and fore-arms were covered in rough flaky patches of skin that she sometimes had to scratch because of the itching. She had a number tattooed on the inside of her wrist that might have been the service number of a hand-some young pilot who was shot down in the First World War and would have married Nanny in a real church, with real bridesmaids, if he had lived.

Nobody knew for sure where Nanny's husband had

174

gone or why he had left home all those years ago. They once had lots of children who grew up to be aunts and uncles whom Frankie did not know, and they in turn had babies who became cousins that Frankie had not met. Smallfry was the youngest of Nanny's children and would never, ever accept those others as her *real* brothers and sisters. Smallfry's father was a mysterious person whom no one had ever seen and whose name had not been written down on her birth certificate. He might have been a Spanish nobleman with red hair and green eyes, or the master of a magnificent foreign sailing ship, or the leader of a band of gypsies who were really princes and princesses in disguise.

His afternoon with Nanny was slow and pleasant. She had made a seedless lemon cake that was dry and powdery in his mouth so that he had to sip a glass of dandelion-and-burdock to help it down. His other nanny made fruit cakes that were moist and heavy, or dense chocolate cakes and buns that he could eat without drinking, but this nanny made everything crumbly and sharp-tasting because she did not have a sweet tooth like Frankie's. He fed some of his cake crumbs to Peter the budgie and agreed with Nanny when she said how well the little fellow was learning to talk. They listened to someone talking and singing on the radio, Nanny dozing in her armchair while Frankie sprawled on the tab rug with his hands clasped behind his head. There was a picture of a dark-eyed baby hanging above the fireplace. This was Budd, who was born a whole year before Frankie and would have been his big brother if only he had not died in hospital when he was just six months old.

The clock on the mantelpiece chimed the quarter, and Nanny's eyes flickered open just as Frankie stooped to kiss her forehead. She patted his hand and smiled at him; and, although he grinned sheepishly and felt his cheeks grow hot, he was not really embarrassed that she had caught him kissing her.

She dabbed at his bitten hand with a wad of cotton-wool dipped in iodine and gave him a solemn warning about going too close to the dog, even when his parents were in the same room. Then it was ten minutes to four and time for her to walk with him along Park Lane and across Little Horton Lane to the corner where the Methodist church stood. Then she held his hand and walked with him all the way down to the Baptist church building on the corner of Trinity Road. She was wearing her Sunday-best coat. It was smooth and grey and fastened with two rows of buttons down the front. A headscarf was knotted under her chin to hide her curling-pins; her shoes were stout and very sensible, her stockings thick and brown with only one ladder which had been neatly sewn up. Everyone could see she was a nice lady, just by looking at her. She always carried one of those big brown handbags with deep pockets on the inside, and a squashy purse that held lots and lots of coins and opened and closed with a loud snap. She handed him a threepenny piece and two pennies for his spending money and a big slice of lemon cake in a brown paper bag. When she kissed him goodbye her lips were soft and warm and her fingers touched him everywhere: on his hair, his cheeks, his shoulders, the collar of his shirt.

'Now, you be a good boy, Frankie,' she said. 'Wait for your mam at the footpath and don't speak to any strange men.'

'No, Nanny.'

'And brush your teeth every night before you go to bed.'

'Yes, Nanny, and thank you for cleaning my shoes.'

'That's all right, dear. Kiss for Nanny?'

When she smiled her eyes creased into hundreds of little wrinkles at the edges. He reached up to clasp his hands around her neck in a big hug, breathing in her smell of face-powder and coal-tar soap. Then he puckered his lips and kissed her noisily, right on the mouth.

He walked all by himself along Trinity Road, where the only houses to be seen were in a short row behind the church and the Sunday school. It took him a long time to reach the narrow walled footpath that divided Trinity Fields on both sides of the road, yet each time he turned around his nanny was there in the distance, blowing kisses and waiting to return his wave.

19

THE WALL surrounding Trinity Fields was much taller
than Frankie, though there were places here and there
where the uneven stones allowed him to climb up and
see over its top. There were five separate fields in all,
three on one side of Trinity road and two on the other.
Of the two nearest to Frankie, one was used as a
common athletics ground, which meant that a large
central rectangle of grass was kept well cut and tidy.
Over the years it had become worn with the pounding
of feet and stained with the marks of a thousand
different activities. This was where the circus came to
stay, where painted trucks and cages arrived as if from
nowhere and the tents sprang up as quickly and
mysteriously as mushrooms in the quiet dawn; where
magic was a way of life, and trapeze artists flew
through the air without wings and every breath was a
sniff of sheer enchantment. This was where Buddie
and his sisters, when they were no bigger than
Frankie, had seen the giraffe-necked women, those
inky-black ladies from darkest Africa whose necks had
been stretched and stretched by silver rings until they
were as long as a man's arm. This was where Captain
Williams, the world-famous black lion-tamer, had
awed the public with his spectacular mixed ring of
lions, tigers, leopards and bears, an act so dangerous
and so sensational that men gasped and women
screamed or fainted at every performance. And later
that same Captain Williams, horribly scarred by claw

and tooth and as terrifying to encounter as a wild African chief, had called for tea at Nanny's in Lansdowne Place with a ravenous appetite for apple pie and a fistful of free tickets for the circus.

Frankie reached the footpath and turned to wave to Nanny for the last time. She was very far away, but he guessed she was smiling as she moved out of sight beyond the Baptist church on the corner. On the opposite side of the road from where he now waited, he could see the middle field, beyond which stood the derelict and spooky Horton Old Hall. Decent folk did not go near the place for fear of ghosts, but Frankie had heard that gypsies and tramps went there at night to light bonfires and drink hard liquor. He pulled his watch from the pocket of his trousers and checked to see that it was still ticking. He had set the hands according to the time on Nanny's chiming mantel-clock. He turned the winder just a little to make sure that it was fully wound, then pushed the watch back into his pocket. It was ten minutes past four. Smallfry would come for him soon.

Stepping into the footpath was like walking into the mouth of a tunnel. The walls seemed to lean inward as if determined to close the gap between the fields. Elegant fireweeds of rich magenta grew up from the long grass and lolled over the tops of the walls like so many gossipy ladies with nodding heads and pretty flowered hats. Smallfry would wait for him at the lower end of the footpath, and Frankie wanted to make sure she was there before he ventured down its winding tunnel-like length. He knew a spot where the wall leaned the other way to allow for a curve in the path. He found it quickly and began to climb, heaving himself up until he straddled the rough stones on the very top of the wall. From there he could see right down the slopes and turns to the lower end of the footpath where it opened out into Easby Road. There was no sign of Smallfry. The road was deserted in both directions except for two slow-moving cyclists and a large brown van with a trailer. He took out his watch again. It was only a quarter past four.

Though he stared and stared, he could not make out the shape of the public callbox squeezed into the farthest corner of the field with its door opening on to Easby Road; yet simply by closing his eyes he could see the circus in all its remembered splendour. He could see the scary clowns with their still, artificial faces, all the more sinister because they could lure even the most reluctant small boys the way moths are sucked into candle-flames. He could see the yellow-eyed tigers and restless lions pacing to and fro across their cages; the huge, lumbering elephants, the prancing ponies, performing dogs and slow stately camels with their measured stride and noble expressions. On the tip of his tongue he could taste the very essence of it all, but when he opened his eyes the sights, sounds and smells of that other world were sucked away on the breezes of a perfectly ordinary afternoon. The field where the circus stayed was empty.

It was not such a steep drop into the left-hand field, where the grass grew tallest and the weeds thickest. After first making sure that he would be able to climb out again, he leaped into the long grass and rolled down a slope with his eyes closed and his hands clasped over his face. He came to a halt where the grass was lush and sweet and very green, with a sprinkling of daisies that reminded him of icing sugar dusted across the top of a birthday cake. He decided to pick the tiny flowers one by one and thread them into a pretty daisy-chain for Smallfry. He was unable to make a slit in the stem with his thumbnail because all his nails were so badly bitten, so he took out his

180

precious nit-comb, ran it through his hair a few times, then used its edge to make the required hole through which to slot each flower. The sweetness of the grass tickled his nose until he sneezed. He sat perfectly still while a butterfly with red and orange wings fluttered about the plucked flowers as if admiring his handiwork. When it settled briefly on his bent knee he held his breath and closed his eyes and made a wish the way he always did if ever he stepped in a rainbow of oil when the road was wet after the rain. From time to time he climbed the wall to watch for Smallfry. At twenty minutes to five he decided to straddle the wall for five whole minutes, hoping to spot her as she rounded the corner from Ashgrove or walked up the road from Morley Street. As he watched the quiet roads and deserted footpath, he tried to remember exactly what she had said, what words she had used when she shared with him her very important secret.

'Your father is thinking of going back to sea. He may decide to rejoin the merchant navy. This is by no means *certain*, of course, but you should prepare yourself for the worst. He *may* have to leave us for a while.'

She had used her cultured voice, her precise and very serious voice, and Frankie had said nothing because her words seemed to go straight to his throat and sit there like a huge hard lump. He hated the way words had so much power and finality; the way small, softly spoken ones could have just as much impact and cause just as much hurt as big shouted ones. Words could make things happen. Just *saying* that Buddie was going away would eventually make it so.

Frankie also knew that words did not always mean exactly what they *seemed* to mean. There were children who thought their dads had joined the merchant navy when everyone else knew they had really been sent to prison for doing something bad, like stealing or

181

spending all their money in the pubs and clubs instead of giving it to their families. Other people talked about them behind their backs and cried shame on them because their mams were drawing Prisoner's Aid or National Assistance. In summer these fatherless children went on special holidays to a place called Heysham Head at Morecambe, near the seaside. They were taken there by the *Cinderella Homes*. Freddie Binns and his sisters had been to Heysham Head three times, for a whole fortnight each time, and they had all come back to school as if they did not care at all about the shame of it. Frankie had heard that they were made to write letters home and call the teachers 'Mum' and 'Dad', and all the girls had to wear gingham dresses in green-and-white or blue-and-white or red-and-white, according to their age. Freddie Binns had collected a whole boxful of pebbles and shells and walked in the sea at Morecambe, and he said the sea was just like in the films only bigger and much colder. Mary Binns had come back as brown as a berry because of the sunshine and sea air and long daily walks in the countryside. Her younger sister, Christine, had learned all the words to a song called 'The Old Lamp-Lighter'. One day she was going to sing it all by herself on the stage of a real concert like the ones they had at Heysham Head. Frankie was not sure about the *Cinderella Homes*. He laughed at Freddie Binns because his dad was in prison, but it was not an easy thing to laugh at someone who had walked on a genuine beach and built sand-castles with a bucket and spade and ridden on a donkey and plunged his whole body into the sea.

Intent on the making of Smallfry's daisy-chain, Frankie sucked in his lower lip and scowled the way his father did to help his concentration. He considered the possibility that Buddie had done something bad and would have to go to court, where a man in a white wig would decide if he should go to prison or be returned to his family. He thought about the sugar that had been tipped from paper sacks into mattress ticking and the opening rolled over and stitched to stop it leaking out. He thought about the butter, cheese and jam that were never to be spoken about to other people, the petrol-coupons and the piles of ration-books in Buddie's locked cupboard, the pigs slaughtered in the cellar and their pieces sold to butchers in shops as far away as Halifax and Leeds. It occurred to him that Buddie might be in serious trouble, or that rationing was about to come to an end, the way Valance Fraser's dad always said it would. He was not sure how Buddie would make a living if the Government put an end to rationing. Perhaps it was time father and son had a man-to-man discussion about the future. Frankie could help. He had his secret hoard of treasures and his precious life savings. He could even sell his watch and his army greatcoat, or pawn them at Dalby's jeweller's shop at the bottom of Manchester Road. He was willing to be parted from everything he possessed if it would raise enough money to keep the family together so that the merchant navy need never be mentioned again.

Frankie fastened off the loop of daisies and turned it in his hands to examine every individual flower. Satisfied that it was perfect, he placed it beside him and lay back in the long grass to stare through narrowed eyes at the deep clear sky. Clouds like wispy bits of vapour hung against the blue. Here and there an insect hovered or a bird flew high on the warm air. A ladybird marched across the back of his hand, so tiny and weightless that he could not feel the touch of her legs against his skin. He blew gently on to her spotted back, watched the tiny transparent wings unfold to carry her away from the intrusion of his breath.

He was warm and comfortable with the sun on his face and the springy bed of grass at his back. He remembered how he had felt when his teacher had told the whole class that his Uncle Dan, eldest of Buddie's two brothers, was one of the boxers appearing in the ring at the Olympia Buildings in Thornton Road. He even remembered being only eight years old, wearing his cowboy suit and riding his pony outside the grounds of Old Ashfield for the very first time. The man from the *Telegraph and Argus* had arrived to take his picture right there in Trinity Road, sitting astride Trigger with Buddie holding the reins. Nobody at school had believed that he was famous until Wally Watmough's mother had brought the newspaper at dinner-time and there he was, 'Rider of the Range', for everyone to see. It did not seem to matter then that he was bottom of the class in spelling and mental arithmetic. His photograph was in the newspaper, and everyone knew he was famous. The excitement of it all could still warm him with secret pleasures and make him smile right down to his belly-button.

'Your father is thinking of going back to sea.'

Smallfry's words suddenly rang out in his mind, scattering the happy imagery and alerting him to the newest danger lurking in the shadowed corners of his life. He could not begin to imagine a world in which Buddie, with his songs and his laughter and his unpredictable moods, did not exist. How would Smallfry, so ill and so brave, cope with everything if Buddie had to go away or really *did* decide to go back in the merchant navy? Who would keep the swaggering Tom Fish from the house? Who would tell the workmen what to do, and show the band which music to play, and sing the songs in that loud Fats Waller voice everyone enjoyed so much? Who would collect all the swill-bins, kill the turkeys and chickens, slaughter the pigs and make the

184

special omelettes from the unlaid eggs? His leaving would be a disaster. Nothing would be the same if Buddie went away. Everything would change, and Frankie would suffer because then the Bogeyman and the Irishman would have the run of the whole house.

Frankie hung the daisy-chain around his neck and climbed back to his position on the very top of the wall. There were two horses in the farthest corner of the field, both standing with their heads over the wall as if hoping for a titbit from some generous passer-by. They held his interest only briefly. It was almost twenty-five minutes to six, and he was beginning to feel concerned because Smallfry was very late and he was not sure what to do. He could find his way home from there, or go back to Nanny's house in Park Road, or walk down Morley Street to the house of his other nanny in Lansdowne Place. He knew he would do none of these things, no matter how late it got, because Smallfry had told him to wait right there, and she would be furious if he caused trouble by disobeying her. He only hoped that she would come before it grew dark. He was afraid to be left all alone in Trinity Fields in the dark.

He had been watching the horses for some time when he noticed the familiar blue van parked just around the corner from the junction of Easby Road and Laisteridge Lane. He was bitterly disappointed. He had wanted her to come alone. Tom Fish would laugh out loud and poke fun at him for making the daisy-chain, and Smallfry would take his side against Frankie just by saying nothing and smiling up at the man in that shy pretty way she had of making other people feel special. After a few minutes he saw her climb from the van, cross the road and walk towards the footpath with her coat billowing behind her and her bright yellow dress catching the sunlight. Frankie's relief that Irish Tom was not going to follow her was short-lived. She turned to wave as the van pulled away, and Frankie felt a stab of pain because she had not turned back with a smile to wave at *him* when she had hurried away from Nanny's house earlier in the day.

He climbed down the steepest side of the wall with great care, clinging like a fly to the jagged stones. He was forced to jump the last few feet where the hedgerow sloped up the wall and the path was worn gully-deep by the passing of many feet. He landed on uneven ground and had to break his fall with both hands and his bottom. Then he thrust his fists deep into his pockets and trudged along the footpath, scowling with resentment and concerned that he might never, in all his life, grow big enough to get his revenge on the Irishman. Smallfry had been away for a whole afternoon, and it had not even occurred to him that she had left him alone in order to meet Tom Fish. Now it pained him even to suspect that they had been together for all those hours, doing private things and perhaps speaking words that would send Buddie away for a long time.

20

'FRANKIE? Where are you, Frankie?'

He was peeing into the hedgerow, aiming an arc of steaming urine at the heads of a clump of thistles, when she called his name from the bottom of the footpath. Her voice sounded light and carefree. It made him smile, but even before he could fasten up his flies and offer a reply she called again in a sharper, more urgent tone.

'Frankie! Where the hell are you?'

'I'm here. I'm coming.'

He fumbled with the top button on his pants and sprinted the last few yards into the final bend of the footpath. She was standing with her back to him, one hand stretched out behind her to halt him in his tracks. She was leaning forward to peep round the corner of the wall as if she feared being seen by someone out in the road.

'What is it?' Frankie asked anxiously. 'What's wrong?'

'It's your father. He's just climbed out of his jeep and now he's standing down the road by the telephone-box. He may have seen me . . . '

'Has he come to take us home?' There was genuine relief in his voice because he knew they would be safe with Buddie. He always went the long way home, and Frankie enjoyed riding in the jeep.

'Hush. Be quiet.'

'Look, Smallfry,' he whispered. 'I made you a necklace out of daisies. They were growing wild in the field and . . . '

She waved him to silence. He heard her suck in a deep breath and hold it for a long time before exhaling in a long heavy sigh. Suddenly she straightened up and used the palms of both hands to smooth the swept-up sides of her hair. She was smiling. She was just like the lady in the film who walked out to meet the police after shooting her treacherous husband six times with his own service revolver. Her back was straight, her head high, her eyes bright and unafraid. She reached out her hand and dropped it lightly on to Frankie's shoulder to steer him through the narrow opening into Easby Road. Now her head was bent towards him, and her green eyes looked closely into his face. She smiled and touched his hair with her free hand, guiding him along the pavement to where Buddie's jeep was parked not a hundred yards away.

'We had a wonderful time today, you and I,' she was saying, with a chilly edge sharpening the sweet tone of her voice. 'We stayed together at Nanny's house until about three-thirty. Then I took you to the park and you played on the swings and watched some children fishing for tiddlers in the pond. Look at me when I'm talking to you, Frankie.'

'Yes, Smallfry.'

'I don't want your father to know we've seen him.'

'No, Smallfry.'

'Now, don't forget to tell him about the ice-lolly you had and the whole glass of lemonade you drank in the park café. It was a lovely sunny day, so instead of coming home early we sat in the grass on the hill near the cricket-field. I stayed in the shade, of course, as I always do. Are you listening to me, Frankie?'

'Yes, Smallfry. Look, I made you a daisy-chain.'

188

'Ah, yes. Very nice.'

She lifted the loop of tiny flowers from around his neck, and he knew by the expression on her face, even before he examined the daisy-chain for himself, that it was spoilt. All the flowers had closed up their petals and gone limp and stringy because they had been too long without water. It was so unfair. She had promised to come for him at a quarter past four and now it was ten to six and all the daisies had died. Tom Fish was to blame for making her so late. It was as if the Irishman knew, even when he was not actually *there*, just how to ruin things for Frankie.

A sudden thought occurred to him when he recalled the pains he had taken in making the daisy-chain. He had used his metal comb to make the slits in the stems, and he could not remember putting it back into his pocket. He dipped his hands into both trouser pockets and sighed with relief. There was his watch and the money Nanny had given him. And there was the special comb from his other nanny, the shiny silver fine-toothed comb that would keep the nits from living in his hair.

'Hi there, you two. Well, well, well. Looks to me like you've been having a great time together.'

Buddie had walked along the road to meet them. His thumbs were stuck down the big leather belt with the fancy brass buckle that he always wore around his waist. The legs of his Yankee-style working pants were tucked into wellington boots whose tops were folded over and held in place by thick woollen socks. He was swaggering and grinning. He looked like a small, brown, freckled cowboy with a glittering gold-edged smile and a hand-rolled cigarette dangling unlit from one corner of his mouth.

'Buddie! What a *lovely* surprise.' Smallfry was aston- ished to see him there. Her eyes widened, and her hands lifted in amazement. 'Look, Frankie, here's your father, come to meet us and take us home. Isn't this a lovely surprise?'

'Yes, Smallfry.'

'Hi-ya, Frankie.' Buddie chuckled and rubbed a crinkly palm over the boy's short spiky hair.

'Hi-ya, Buddie,' Frankie returned the grin.

'Oh, Buddie, we've had a really *wonderful* day,' Smallfry exclaimed with a happy sigh. 'Isn't that so, Frankie dear?'

Frankie nodded his head. 'I made a daisy-chain for Smallfry, but it died.'

'Well, now, never you mind too much about that, boy. It's the thought behind the gift that really counts. I'm sure your mam will be just as pleased you made it for her, even if it *did* go and die before you could get it home.'

'We were in the park for *hours*,' Smallfry said, smoothing the hair at the nape of her neck. 'We really enjoyed ourselves, didn't we, Frankie?'

Frankie nodded again. 'Nanny gave me a big piece of lemon cake to bring home. It's here in my jacket pocket. I'll let you share it with me, if you like.'

'You bet,' Buddie said in a very loud voice. 'Equal shares, sliced dead centre, right down the middle. OK?'

'You bet,' Frankie mimicked, grinning.

'Hey, kid, are you too big to hold your dad's hand?'

'No, sir.'

Buddie stuck out his hand, and Frankie reached for it eagerly. He felt the short hard fingers close around his and the dry callused palm scrape against his own. It was a big hand, strong and brown and familiar. It felt good.

'And not too big to hold the hand of his favourite lady, I hope,' Smallfry said in her nicest, kindest voice.

'Oh, no, Smallfry.' Frankie beamed with pleasure and wiped his fingers on his trousers before taking the hand she offered. It was pale and soft and so light that he felt he must hold it very tightly to prevent it slipping from his grip.

Frankie knew the kids at school would make fun of him if he was seen walking along the road between his parents like one of the infants, holding hands. They would call him a cissy and a mammy's boy, but for once he did not really care about Wally Watmough and Freddie Binns and Valance Fraser and all the other kids at St Andrew's. He wanted to hold on to this moment for as long as he possibly could, because somehow he knew that it was special.

Out of the corner of his eye he saw something move and turned his head to see that Smallfry had dropped the withered daisy-chain. It lay on the pavement in an untidy coil. It was hard to imagine that it had ever been pretty, yet just a short time ago those flowers had been growing in the field with their petals wide open and their delicate little faces turned to the sun. Frankie did not mind that she had thrown the chain away, because no fine and beautiful lady could be expected to wear, or even carry in her hand, such a sorry gift. He glanced up at his parents, at the colourful real-life American and the gorgeous Hollywood film-star, and he thought he must be the luckiest, most privileged boy in the country. Whatever changes and new experiences he sensed were looming somewhere beyond the limits of his comprehension, for the present, for the precious here-and-now, Frankie was content.

He saw Buddie close one eye in a huge wink that made Smallfry's face light up with one of her brilliant smiles, and he wished the moment could stay and not vanish or fade and die the way the daisies had done. He did not want anything to change. He wanted everything in his life to remain exactly as it was right then, with his whole world as sunny and as warm as the day itself, with no darkness, no lurking shadows, and no Bogeyman.